VISA FOR AVALON

VISA FOR

AVALON

A NOVEL BY BRYHER

INTRODUCTION BY SUSAN MᶜCABE

PARIS
PRESS
Ashfield, Massachusetts 2004

Library of Congress Cataloguing-in-Publication Data
Bryher, 1894-1983
Visa for Avalon / Bryher ; with an introduction by Susan McCabe.
    p. cm.
Includes bibliographical references.
ISBN 1-930464-07-X (alk. paper)
1. Totalitarianism--Fiction.   I. Title.

PR6003.R98V57   2004
823'.914--dc22

                                        2004016116

a b c d e f g h i j

Printed in the United States of America.

VISA FOR AVALON

A NOTE FROM THE PUBLISHER

I FIRST READ *Visa for Avalon* eight years ago, as part of a winter reading jag with my friend Mary Lucas. From January through March of 1996, we moved through all of Bryher's historical novels, her memoirs, and *Visa for Avalon*. Since then, haunted by its prescient warning of the devastating effects of political apathy, I placed *Visa for Avalon* on the shelf beside my desk where I could see it, hoping that Paris Press would be able to bring this vital novel back into print at some point in the future.

Recent restrictions on civil liberties imposed by the Patriot Act turned my thoughts once more to *Visa for Avalon,* and inspired the Press to publish the book at this time. During the production of *Visa for Avalon,* we re-discovered an essay by Walter Benjamin, a contemporary of Bryher's whom she supported during the outbreak of World War II. The essay, "Theses on the Philosophy of History," suggests that it is essential to be mindful of the past and to pursue a proactive engagement with history. Benjamin's sentiment goes hand-in-hand with Bryher's "novel of warning" (as Horace Gregory so aptly

described the book when it was first published). By present-
ing *Visa for Avalon* as an allegory, Bryher offers a story that
can be applied to any time and any country.

The Paris Press edition of *Visa for Avalon* closely repli-
cates the 1965 Harcourt, Brace & World edition of the novel.
The Press added an introduction by Susan McCabe, this pub-
lisher's note, and a biography of Bryher. In a few instances,
Paris Press has corrected spelling and punctuation for general consistency.

I am deeply grateful to the Estate of W. Bryher for grant-
ing Paris Press permission to reissue this important novel.
Paris Press offers thanks to Timothy Schaffner, Valentine
Schaffner, and the Schaffner Family Foundation for their support and their help in understanding both Bryher's life and
work. We owe immense thanks to Susan McCabe for her fine
introduction and biographical information about Bryher.
Thank you, Emily Wojcik, for your bountiful and valuable
assistance throughout every stage of this production. This
edition would not exist without your editorial skills, intel-
lect, and overall good cheer. Thanks also to Margery Adams,
Anne Goldstein, Jeff Oaks, Theo Oktenberg, Barney Saltz-
berg, Eva Schocken, and Stephanie Schoen for assistance and
feedback; to Richard Lilly and Laurie Magriel for inspiring
suggestions about the cover of the book, and to Allison Ryan
for the beautiful photograph. Thank you to Ann R. Stokes,
the Schocken Family Foundation, Peggy Shumaker and Joseph

Usibelli, the Massachusetts Cultural Council, and Joan Heller, Diane Bernard, and the Astraea Foundation for the enthusiasm and generous support that made the publication of this book possible. Special thanks to Jeff Potter and Lisa Clark for the beautiful design of the book. And finally, thank you to Susan Stanford Friedman for *Psyche Reborn,* which introduced me to H.D.'s life and work, and led me to Bryher.

In a time when liberty and democracy are at risk, Bryher reminds us that inertia, apathy, and complacency only fuel the political forces that can strip us of the rights we so often take for granted. Paris Press hopes you will agree that such a message is necessary and useful now, and we are honored to bring *Visa for Avalon* back into the public eye.

JAN FREEMAN

ix

INTRODUCTION

"PEOPLE LIKE US have no rights anymore," one of Bryher's characters exclaims in *Visa for Avalon*.¹ Bryher's futuristic vision is at once a call to action and an elegy for a democratic way of life. In a lyric and mesmerizing style, *Visa for Avalon* presents the effects that a totalitarian "Movement" has on familiar citizens in a remarkably familiar country where free speech, independence, and homeland are exchanged for the supposed betterment of the population. The homogenizing mass culture of linoleum, chain stores, super highways, and factories — the more innocuous effects of this oppressive government — appear to have arisen overnight like a "protein" from "outer space."² Bryher depicts "Big Brother" on an intimate scale, combining a stark panic with the urgency encountered in writers such as Franz Kafka and Margaret Atwood. Insofar as it operates in the tradition of George Orwell and Aldous Huxley, with their nightmare visions of industrial and totalitarian societies, *Visa for Avalon* provides a more compressed, perhaps more human, rendering of the threats to freedom that every generation must face. Bryher builds suspense through the very last page, questioning whether exile is the only possible means of protest and route to safety in response to the seemingly unstoppable force of "the Movement."

The work of Bryher (1894–1983), a pioneer whose life serves as a model of personal and cultural defiance, has fallen out of print, which makes this new edition a momentous occasion. With the exception of her early coming-of-age novels, *Development* and *Two Selves,* published in one volume by The University of Wisconsin Press (2000),[3] Bryher's writing has been unavailable for nearly thirty years. In addition to *Visa for Avalon,* Bryher's literary output includes eight historical novels, which received great critical acclaim in the fifties and sixties; two romans à clef; three memoirs, *West* (her 1924 account of her travel to America), *The Heart to Artemis: A Writer's Memoir,* and *The Days of Mars: A Memoir 1940–45*; and two volumes of poetry.

In the last twenty years, Bryher's name has appeared most frequently in connection with Imagist poet H.D. (Hilda Doolittle), who was her partner from 1919 until H.D.'s death in 1961. Bryher is also known for her monetary support and patronage of many modernist writers, artists, philosophers, and cultural icons, such as Marianne Moore, Dorothy Richardson, Sylvia Beach and Adrienne Monnier, the psychoanalyst Hanns Sachs, members of Sigmund Freud's family, Eslanda and Paul Robeson, and Robert Herring. She founded

Contact Publishing Company (with her first husband, Robert McAlmon), showcasing experimental writers such as Gertrude Stein, James Joyce, and Mina Loy; the first English film journal, *Close Up* (with her second husband, Kenneth Macpherson), which sought to unite progressive film criticism with politics; and *Life and Letters To-day,* featuring writers ranging from Franz Kafka and Paul Valéry to Muriel Rukeyser, Elizabeth Bishop, and Edith Sitwell.

During the thirties, in the face of Hitler's rise to power, Bryher helped over 100 Jewish and German intellectuals (among them many psychoanalysts), university students, and children flee Nazi persecution and in many cases secure visas. One of the few individuals she assisted but who could not, at the last moment, safely escape was the cultural philosopher Walter Benjamin, who killed himself in despair and exhaustion at the Franco-Spanish border when he was prevented from crossing.[4] Bryher herself was forced to flee Switzerland in 1940 and upon her exodus she burned all of her records identifying refugees. This anticipates the consul in *Visa for Avalon,* who burns all the office files before vacating "the City."[5]

Visa for Avalon takes place in one week, during which Bryher's characters quickly abandon their homes and encounter crowds, roadblocks, and the authorities in their quest to acquire the last remaining visas for Avalon. Robinson, a retired businessman, helps his elderly landlady Lilian Blunt depart from the sleepy fishing village of Trelawney after a "horrid little man" from the Movement evicts her from her Rose Cottage to make way for a new highway. Purposely vague, *Visa for Avalon* presents the eerie outlines of *any* totalitarian government that claims to act on behalf of the population's "common needs" through so-called technological and social advancement, while stripping people of their rights and individual voices.

The first signs of the Movement emerge with imagist brilliance: a young girl sporting a signature button and "wearing a green windbreaker in one of the shiny, new materials"[6] searches for her "party" at the seaside. Clearly a member of one of the youth groups that has newly infiltrated Trelawney, she accosts Robinson. Bryher compares her to an "amorphous stranded jellyfish." The group's leader is "a woman whose lips turned down till they almost met her chin, giving an impression of being a fishhook upside down." Lest we think the Movement refers to unruly teenagers or the liberal protestors of the early 1960s, Bryher depicts it as mindless, rigid obedience to authority possible at any moment in history: the group marches "like a long green caterpillar with many legs and one rudimentary brain."[7]

By the time Bryher wrote *Visa for Avalon*, she had published seven well-received historical novels in England and the U.S. However in 1965, while Helen Wolff at Harcourt was publishing and promoting *Visa for Avalon* in America, Bryher's editor Adrian House at Collins in London hesitated to release a British edition. Bryher responded with characteristic honesty, beginning her response with a curt: "Come off it."[8] When further pressed about his reluctance, House suggested that readers would not readily enjoy anything from Bryher other than her transfigurations of the past: "Their acceptance, their recognition, of the world you have created for them has been absolute. Will they now recognize or accept themselves as they are portrayed in the near future?"[9] Bryher suspected that House was squeamish about the "politics" of the book, believing that readers might recognize themselves all too clearly, rather than not at all. After all, while Bryher's historical novels do indeed recreate the past with vivid force and color (from the Romans of *Coin of Carthage* to the Renaissance courts of *The Player's Boy*), the "today" of *Visa for Avalon* is similarly visceral and close.

In any case, Bryher did not disappoint her faithful readers. The novel's reference to the Isle of Avalon in Arthurian legend recalls the historical mode readers had come to expect from her. The reference is complex, however. In more than one version of the legend, King Arthur comes to the "island of apples" (the Celtic meaning of Avalon) to die, a place that the 10th-century cleric Geoffrey of Monmouth describes as a feminine idyll where "the earth of its own accord brings forth... all things in superabundance."[10] In Geoffrey's telling, Arthur seeks to be healed, but in Sir Thomas Malory's "La Morte d'Arthur," published 300 years later, such rehabilitation is an illusion. After "foaming at the mouth," Arthur is borne away to Avalon, where he is greeted by women who "wept and shrieked," and among whom he dies.[11] Other legends depict Avalon as a beautiful netherworld of sorts, where Arthur lives in immortality.[12]

This duality between a paradise and the ominous shadow of death colors the characters' own escape in *Visa for Avalon*. Alex, an employee of the consulate who helps Robinson and Lilian secure visas, was once a resident of Avalon and is deeply ambivalent about returning. Likewise, Lilian's own knowledge of the island is limited to the foreboding caveat that "nobody who landed there ever returned."[13] However, the island appeals to her because it is "utterly different," unlike the more common destinations of America and New Zealand.[14]

None of us is exempt from the ravages of history. Bryher lived through two World Wars as well as the beginning of the Cold War before writing *Visa for Avalon*. For the better part of the 20th century, she witnessed the destruction of Europe and the galvanic political upheavals that violently called into question an unquestioning faith in progress and technology. In the wake of Nazism and Stalin's brutal rule in Russia, the Cold War brought forth other forms of repression: the Iron Curtain, the Cultural Revolution in Maoist China, and the McCarthy witch hunts in America, to name several of the most prominent examples that haunt this compelling tale. Bryher's activism before World War II and the traumatic experience of living through the blitz in London (the subject of her novel *Beowulf*) amplified her hope that fiction might teach us essential historic truths that could stimulate better social decisions. With the accuracy of one who experienced the raids and ruins of London first-hand, she revisits the constant terror that everything one loves could be destroyed in an instant. *Visa for Avalon* asks: "Could a lifetime disappear as utterly as this?"[15]

In the June 1933 issue of *Close Up*, Bryher's article "What Shall You Do in the War?" reports the startling facts (primarily suppressed from the news) that were intended to compel her readers to take action and which led to her activist role in assisting forced exiles:

> Hundreds of Jewish doctors have been forbidden to practise and have been dismissed from the hospitals. They are unable to obtain work and in several cases known to me personally, they have been left to starve. Einstein and many of their best scientists are in exile. Those who waited too long, or could not afford a railway ticket, are shot or are in prison.... It is quite possible that a lot of German citizens do not realize what is happening. If a man complains of his treatment or of the new laws, he is beaten to death or sent to a concentration camp.[16]

The Berlin that Bryher knew in the twenties as a cultural center abruptly morphed into a "city where police cars and machine guns raced about the streets, where groups of brown uniforms waited at each corner. The stations had been crowded with people whose bundles, cases or trunks bulged with household possessions."[17] This description reappears in *Visa for Avalon*: people wait for buses that will never arrive, the streets clog with check-points, and the characters experience "the unreasoning terror that came in jerks and ebbed away again."[18]

The first fugitives from the Nazis started to arrive at Bryher's home in 1933. She described their struggle: "Suppose that you were a citizen of good standing... Then overnight you were declared an enemy, beaten up, your possessions seized and if you were very, very lucky, allowed to leave with your family... for an alien land where your professional qualifications were useless."[19]

The narrative cannot be divorced from the transformation of Bryher's home in Switzerland into a "receiving station" for immigrants. Like Alex in *Visa for Avalon*, she did anything she could to help citizens escape. The novel captures the sense of cataclysmic changes occurring as if "overnight," but underscores that no political change occurs without the refusal, at least on some level, of people to see and respond to the signs.

Visa for Avalon, by refusing to specify its horror, evokes a situation that we understand: roadblocks, suppression of free speech, the real possibility of incarceration, the nightmare of captivity in a world where rights are eroded and laws (except those fabricated to suit the powers that be) are meaningless, a rogue government that calls itself a legitimate one. In this upside-down world, Augier, an auguring pilot, knows that "it is well within the power of the Movement to seize the plane and intern them all. He suspected that they would merely laugh at international law."[20]

With surreal detachment, *Visa for Avalon* recreates the dislocations that rose with Fascism. That Bryher does not exclusively focus on this element is one of the book's brilliant attributes, for her purposes lie elsewhere. Throughout her writings, Bryher expresses her disgust for totalitarianism, and she also targets apathy. When asked how the new government or "Movement" could have gained so much power, one character in *Visa for Avalon* responds: "It's been in the air for years. But who did anything about it?"[21] Even as he questions what has singled him out as deserving of rescue, Robinson bitterly acknowledges, "People are apathetic until it becomes too late."[22] In *The Heart to Artemis*, Bryher rued her own Cassandra-like role (no one heeded her repeated warnings about the Nazis):

It did not help me when I stood among the ruins of blitzed London to know that my forebodings had come true. I remain ashamed of the majority of my fellow citizens and convinced that apathy is the greatest sin of life. If Europe had reacted with horror to the murder of both the Jews and many other honest German citizens in 1933, the regime would have collapsed.[23]

Bryher brings to history the kind of urgency and crisis that she learned from cinema: we must try to take hold of our fragmented experience and remake it as we would a film, to unsettle apathetic sensibilities and imagine new ways of being. Modernization is not itself the culprit, nor the specter of consumer culture (nor linoleum, which is so omnipresent in *Visa for Avalon* that even a woman in a teashop wears a cap "of white linoleum with an edging of coral beads").[24] Rather it is the use of the modern at the expense of humanity and democratic values that endangers us. *Visa for Avalon* situates us at the threshold of a new dark age, asking us to take seriously threats to our individuality and to our freedom.

SUSAN MCCABE
JULY 3, 2004

NOTES

1 Bryher, *Visa for Avalon* (Ashfield, MA: Paris Press, Inc., 2004), p. 20.

2 Ibid., p. 133.

3 *Bryher: Two Novels: Development and Two Selves*, ed. Joanne Winning (Madison, WI: The University of Wisconsin Press, 2000).

4 For more information, see Hannah Arendt's "Introduction: Walter Benjamin: 1892-1940" in Walter Benjamin's *Illuminations: Essays and Reflections*, ed. Hannah Arendt (New York: Schocken Books, Inc., 1968), p. 1–55.

5 Bryher, *Visa for Avalon* (Ashfield, MA: Paris Press, Inc., 2004), p. 67.

6 Ibid., p. 7.

7 Ibid., p. 44.

8 Bryher to Adrian House, 5 July 1965, Beinecke Rare Book and Manuscript Library, Yale University, New Haven, CT.

9 Adrian House to Bryher, 14 July 1965, Beinecke Rare Book and Manuscript Library, Yale University, New Haven, CT.

10 Geoffrey Ashe, *Mythology of the British Isles* (London: Methuen London, 1990), p. 262.

11 Reprinted in *Arthur King of Britain*, ed. Richard L. Brengle (New York: Appleton-Century-Crofts, 1964), p. 317–319.

12 Arthur Cotterell, *Cassell Illustrated Encyclopedia of Myths & Legends* (London: Cassell, 1989), p. 187.

13 Bryher, *Visa for Avalon* (Ashfield, MA: Paris Press, 2004), p. 24.

14 Ibid., p. 21.

15 Ibid., p. 81.

16 Bryher, "What Shall You Do in the War?," *Close Up*, X.2 (June 1933): p. 189.

[17] Ibid., p. 188.

[18] Bryher, *Visa for Avalon* (Ashfield, MA: Paris Press, Inc., 2004), p. 90.

[19] Bryher, *The Heart to Artemis: A Writer's Memoirs* (New York: Harcourt, Brace & World, Inc., 1962), p. 275.

[20] Bryher, *Visa for Avalon* (Ashfield, MA: Paris Press, Inc., 2004), p. 126.

[21] Ibid., p. 81.

[22] Ibid., p. 18.

[23] Bryher, *The Heart to Artemis: A Writer's Memoirs* (New York: Harcourt, Brace & World, Inc., 1962), p. 276.

[24] Bryher, *Visa for Avalon* (Ashfield, MA: Paris Press, Inc., 2004), p. 43.

VISA FOR AVALON

VISA FÖR AVALON

ONE

HE WOKE TO the sound of the sea.

There was the smell of salt in the air and if it had not been so late in the summer, he would have sworn a tang of chamomile as well. Tang, that was also part of the handle of a sword. He looked round the room and a wave of gratitude rushed through his mind, the moor, the beach, the cawing of the gulls, were not sights and sounds to be snatched at during a three weeks' holiday, he need never leave Trelawney again unless he wished. There was no need to hurry, to rush out one last time to stare at the yellow markings on the old, gray wall and feel under the sharpest impression the grubbing thought that he would have to catch the early train on the following morning in order to be back punctually at the office on Monday. Some might tell him he was stepping backwards; he could show anyone the spot where he had first smelt chamomile as a child and sworn to be a fisherman and live and die in the village. Everything seemed to swim back to a moment when he had been half his present size and living through a time the scents had preserved to give it back to him now on his retirement. Yes, he could feel himself lying, face downward, under a bush again, sniffing the ripe blackberries. It was the savage still alive in man, he supposed, when the ability to distinguish smells was part of being able to keep alive.

He looked at his watch. It would be half an hour before Mrs. Blunt tapped at his door to tell him that breakfast was waiting in the sitting room. He would have liked it earlier himself, not only because he had been a country child but also because during his working days he had wakened early, soon after dawn. The day was work, the night was sleep, but during the hours between six and nine he had been alone with himself and free.

Sometime, but there was no need to hurry, he would have to look for a place of his own. In the meantime, he was contented to be at Rose Cottage and Mrs. Blunt's lodger, partly because it gave him the illusion of its being a prolonged summer holiday, having so often stayed with her before, and also, he supposed, due to a not unreasonable laziness after the fixed hours in the office. He even had an affection for his room, with a square window cut into a thick wall and the ledge under it where he could pile his books. He dared not move the photograph of Mrs. Blunt's terrier that had recently died of old age, although it faced his bed, but he was getting used to it and to the second drawer that always stuck when he wanted to get out a shirt. They were trifles that made this

time seem real. Another wave of gratitude swept over him
again that the sails, the seas and the fields were not a holiday
landscape, lent to him for a few days, but a place where every
nerve found its complement in stalk or water or stone.

He must have drowsed off to sleep because he was
wakened by a sharp knock, "Breakfast's ready, Mr. Robinson, when you are."

Mrs. Blunt always warned him a few minutes in advance
as she hated, she said, "the tea getting cold," and by the time
he had dressed in his roughest fishing clothes and hurried
downstairs, remembering to stoop so as not to bump his head
against a beam, she was just putting his rashers of bacon on
the sitting room table. She, herself, took her egg in the kitchen.
He had suggested joining her there but she had refused. Perhaps she also wanted to be alone?

Lilian! How well the name suited her, although if he
had said this to his city friends and they had seen her, they
would have smiled. Her plump form seemed about to burst
from the shapeless smock that had shrunk after many wash-
ings and her face was as tanned and wrinkled as any fisherman's cheeks. Yet the graces were hers, an unobtrusive
kindliness and independence that caused her sometimes to
bend in a storm like the roses in the tiny garden but not
to break. He had never dared address her as other than
Mrs. Blunt although he had been coming here for holidays for years. His present status was one of life's major

triumphs. "Well, Mr. Robinson, we'll try it for a while and see how we get on but I've never taken lodgers before through the winter."

Today was not even autumn, it was still hot and his friend Alex had invited him out for a day's fishing. "What's it going to be like?" he asked, venturing as far as the kitchen door; she was usually accurate about the weather.

"Better on the water than on land, it's going to be warm."

"Can I get anything for you in the village? I haven't to be at the quayside before ten."

"No, thank you," her English was clear and formal with hardly a trace of dialect. "I have to go in myself. Who's taking you today, Pendean?"

"No, we're going with Bill. Pendean's off lobstering."

"Have you got the satchel for your lunch?"

"I remembered it this time."

"And the thermos?"

He handed them both to her in triumph, wondering how long it would take before she reminded him that he had once, once in more than thirty times, forgotten them. "Mind you don't bring a lot of fish back with you," she scolded, packing the already prepared sandwiches into the box, "I don't mind frying you a couple of pollock for breakfast but I don't like fish myself."

"Last time we hardly caught anything."

"The fishing isn't like it used to be when I was a child. Some say it was the mines in the wars. How much longer has your friend got?"

"It's his last day, they've altered the time of his train and to get his connection, he has to leave tomorrow to be at work on Monday. It's a pity he can't take the Sunday train as usual."

"Change, change, why can't they leave things alone. Not that I am entirely against the modern world. I appreciate my cleaner and the detergents save me a lot of time."

Robinson picked up his satchel and opened the door, "I'll be eating at the Dragon with my friend tonight but I won't be late."

"If you are, I'll leave the key in the usual place. Have a good day, this weather won't last over the weekend."

THE LIFE OF THE village revolved round the harbor. Robinson liked to get there early, there was so much to watch. The fishermen left soon after it was light but a couple of the older men ran two excursion launches during the summer. They were hardly more than barges but the people who stayed at Trelawney wanted to get out on the sea as well as look at it and some of them also hired a boat in the evenings for a bit of fishing. He found a seat for himself on the low wall near the steps where the group had formed to board the

Atlantic Queen. At this late moment of the season she looked as if she could do with a new coat of paint and the two old tires along her sides to keep her from rubbing against the stones were almost worn to shreds.

"You meet people," the girl's skirt billowed in the wind like a strip of wallpaper covered with roses, "then they go off on a reef somewhere and you never see them again till evening."

Reef? What had put that word into her mind? Some magazine story about the South Seas? There were a few submerged rocks to the west of the Point but it was hardly an adequate description of the grassy islet where they landed the passengers for picnics.

"It's perfectly true."

"No, I don't think I shall come here again for a holiday. Not after that sail yesterday. When you're so turned over, it upsets you and puts you off the place a bit."

"I think it's lovely, absolutely lovely."

"Oh yes, it is." The third girl had a camera in her hand and the big white poppies on her red dress were a little startling. It was as if the colors had been reversed in the wash.

"Ready?" The tourists began to feel their way down the slippery steps, a lunch bag jolting against a shoulder or a paper container dangling from a wrist. In the middle of the harbor a small boy was trying to row what seemed to be a barrel rather than a craft and a dozen gulls were snatching bits of dead fish from the beach. It was mixed as all in life was and a new sensation for Robinson to be able to take his place among the natives without joining the crowd.

"Have you seen my party?" A girl broke his meditation without a word of greeting or apology. She faced him angrily, her back to the sea.

"What party?" She was wearing a green windbreaker in one of the shiny, new materials that made her look as amorphous as a stranded jellyfish, but he noticed that she had a round black disk or button on her chest. She must be from one of the youth groups, he supposed, although he had never heard of any in Trelawney before.

"We were just leaving the bus," the girl continued, ignoring his question, "and a cart came up in the opposite direction. I must have taken the wrong turning," she looked anxiously along the quay, "but this is where we were to meet."

"Don't worry, the others will be along in a moment."

"The Movement would not like us to be alone with these idlers here."

The Movement? He had read about it vaguely in the papers but after a lifetime spent in keeping in touch with the news, since his retirement he had sometimes let a week go by without glancing at the headlines. The girl was certainly rude. The tourists might be noisy and blatant as to colors but they had earned their holidays, they had a right to be happy. "There they are!" The girl gave a squeal of relief and darted off to meet a group in the same green coats, coming round the corner. They passed quite close to him, led by a woman whose lips turned down till they almost met her chin, giving an impression of being a fishhook upside down. They did not go to the end of the quay but turned off along a narrow path leading towards the shore.

Robinson turned back to look at the boats but the incident, trivial as it was, made him uneasy. It must be a school but an unpleasant one and it had momentarily destroyed his pleasure in the day. He tried to forget it in watching the second lot of tourists who were waiting for the *Dawn*. For some reason, although he could not distinguish the difference, the boat was said to take more serious passengers than the *Queen*, although the man balancing a tripod on the shoulder of his canary and white striped jacket that looked like a pajama top, did not inspire him with confidence.

"Where are you going tomorrow?" a fisherman bellowed.

"Going 'ome." A boy waved back gaily as he clattered down the steps.

"That's a terrible thought."

Everyone was gay, the youth was making the most of his last excursion without grumbling, it was such a contrast to the dreary discipline of the girls in green jackets who were now marching two by two along the beach.

"Hello!" Alex, masterful and late as ever, strolled down the quay as if he were the harbor master himself. It delighted him to tease Robinson, who was always too early, by arriving at the last possible moment at the boat. "Bill's waiting for us at the other steps so that we can get away in front of the *Dawn*. He thinks there's a good chance this morning off the Ledges."

"It had better be, it's your last day." Robinson picked up his lunch satchel that looked like a poor relation beside his friend's well-filled rucksack.

"There's still a lot of people here, considering it's the end of the season."

"Yes, most of the inns are full. But tell me, Alex, do you know anything about what they call the Movement?"

"Have you stopped listening to the news on principle, just because you've retired?"

"A girl came up to me just now with one of their buttons on her coat and I thought she was very rude."

"I suppose it has not dawned on you that they are threatening to call a General Strike next week."

"But who are they? And what is it?"

"It began among a few disgruntled citizens and has spread virulently, particularly among the young. It's a return to barbarism, I suppose, we have given them more than their little brains can stand."

"What do you mean?"

"A friend of mine told me once that revolutions rose from pushing undigested knowledge into brains unable to absorb it."

"But you don't think we are going to have trouble…" It seemed inconceivable in the sun and air of this gay morning.

"I don't know," then Alex disengaged himself from the strap of his rucksack and handed it down to the waiting fisherman, as if he, too, wanted to absorb himself in the day, "like yourself, I'm leaving politics alone till I get back to the office."

LILIAN BLUNT WALKED down the path, inspecting each plant in turn. Most of them had originally been gifts because money had never been plentiful enough to spend much on the garden. The rosemary was scorched, it simply would not grow where there was too much salt, although Mrs. Brentford at the other end of the village had almost a hedge of it but there was a second crop of roses by the gate, the ones Mr. Robinson had brought her; she wondered if he knew that it was his gift every year of a plant or two or a few seeds, that had made her accept him as a winter lodger? She could not always follow his strange views but he was pleasant, undemanding and out a good deal. She put her basket firmly on the ground and had started to pick some beans when the gate rattled and she looked up to see a white-faced, city-dressed stranger, standing in front of her. "There's no bell," he complained, exactly as if he were a policeman taking somebody's name for not having a light on his cycle.

"We don't need one here." He was probably one of those hire purchase people, wanting to sell her a sweeper.

"Does this cottage belong to a Mrs. Blunt?"

"I'm Mrs. Blunt and it does."

"Then I have a communication for you." He handed her a buff envelope and she had a premonition that if she did not open it, nothing would happen. He stared at her, she fumbled a moment and then slit it open with a finger although normally she would have fetched a paper-knife because she hated torn edges. Perhaps it was something to do with the new reservoir that they had promised the village for years but when she tried to read the form the words danced in front of her and she could hardly put the letters together.

"I will answer any questions you like to put to me." She stared at the official, he had the fixed jaws of a recently dead fish.

"Come in," she led the way into the house. "What does all this mean?"

"It's like this, Mrs. Blunt. The Government is putting up an electricity station at Treworthen. You must have felt the lack of communication here. Thought of moving perhaps..."

"I was born here, widowed here and I expect to die in my cottage."

"This is a dying village, I'm afraid."

"Rubbish, we grow potatoes and we fish, we may not be rich but..."

"There's no work for the young people and when the new station is built there will be factories. Several firms have consulted us about the possibilities and it's almost certain that one of the big cement concerns will start work here."

"But what has all this got to do with me?" Lilian said stupidly.

"We are going to build a new road to Treworthen and I am afraid it will pass across your house. Our surveyor will be here next week and then we can tell you approximately when you have to move. We shall be glad to do anything in our power to help you find another. Perhaps you have relatives elsewhere in the county?"

"I am not going to sell my house."

"There is a Requisition Order for the land, Mrs. Blunt. I assure you, you will receive adequate compensation."

"Put a road across the place where I have spent a lifetime?"

Very narrow, very narrow, the official thought, staring at the tips of his shoes. He hated dealing with these elderly women, they had had no collective training and all that mattered to them was sentiment.

"You must think of the young, the factories will provide a lot of jobs for them. Besides, although it seems hard to you now, we find our people resettle very comfortably."

The only thing that Lilian could think of at that moment was what her father would have felt if he could have heard such news? His savings had gone into the rafters and these bricks, week by week, and year by year. "There must be a right of appeal," she said angrily, "you can't break people's lives up just like this."

"We shall not be touching the West Cliff, perhaps you can find a cottage there."

"I am going to appeal."

He would have liked to tell her that it was a pure waste of money because it was unreasonable to suppose that her claim would be considered with several factories and the Government itself on the opposite side, but he had been trained to leave immediately before saying anything that angry tenants could bring up in or out of Court. "You will find the address and the procedure on the back of the form. Good morning," he picked up his hat and walked briskly down the path.

Lilian sat staring at a china dog that another summer lodger had given her and that she knew that Mr. Robinson did not like. The poor man. He would have to find other lodgings as well and he loved Trelawney as if he were a native of the place. Factories! That meant there would be litter all over the banks of ragged robin and honeysuckle that she had often felt were like a garden, noise at night and perhaps fighting in the village street. She tried to erase the memory of the squat little figure from her mind but it was the climbing rose that kept bringing the interview back to her mind, she could not remember when she had planted it and now it would have to be grubbed up. Her basket was lying there, half full of beans, and it would do no good to leave them in the sun but she could not get on with her tasks, it seemed as if the scrubbing and planting and nursing of the fifty years that she had been alive were without meaning or value. All the same, obeying the instinctive actions of a lifetime, she fetched the basket, put it on the table and hung her apron on its hook, before marching firmly down the road to call on Mabel Ashford, her oldest friend.

MABEL WAS STANDING beside a pail full of kitchen cloths and hanging them, one by one, on the line that ran across a piece of worn grass. Unlike her friend, she had never bothered about her garden. There was a climbing rose over the porch but it had already flowered and the only one of her sons left at home had a patch of potatoes at the back of the cottage. "Why, Lilian, it's nice to see you so early in the day. But what's happened, are you ill?" Mrs. Blunt's face seemed to have faded, as she described it afterwards, and she was staring in front of her as if she had never been inside the place before.

"I've had a shock."

"Has something happened to Mr. Robinson?" With the age-old instinct of the villagers, she looked out to the sea.

"No, he's fishing. I'm glad he isn't here. Not till I've had time to collect my thoughts a bit. I was picking my beans in the garden because today's my day to go into the shops when a horrid little man opened my gate and walked in."

"You don't say! Didn't he even knock?"

"He asked my name and if I owned the cottage."

"I suppose he came about the rates?"

"No, Mabel, no, he said he represented the Government or something and they are going to bulldoze it, he said, to make a new road."

"My dear."

"My father built it and then I was there with Harry, it's been in our hands forty years."

"I did hear something about a road yesterday at the butcher's. One of the Carters was in there. She said they had had an inquiry but they wouldn't mind moving. The daughter's married and has gone up country and they thought they would get quite a lot in compensation."

"Rose Cottage is all I have." It was the whole of a lifetime, running back from school and her mother giving her a piece of seed cake that nobody ever made anymore, she did not quite know why, and Harry, the pride he had had in his boat and his long, lingering death.

"Come inside, my dear, and I'll make you a cup of tea. They can't come and take a person's property away from them without their agreeing to it."

"Do you think so?" It was a facile comfort of the moment only, underneath Lilian knew that she was beaten and would have to leave.

"It will be all right, dear, don't you worry."

What else could she do, Lilian wondered? At one moment of a summer morning she was out picking beans and everything was going on as usual, and then, it had not taken even a minute, she had been pulled up by the roots. She was so dazed that she wondered idly if it were the docks, the groundsel and the thistles that she had grubbed up so lightheartedly and flung onto a bonfire, that had suddenly revenged themselves? Lose her cottage, move to a strange village, no, how could it have happened to her?

"Well, Mabel, what's your news?" It was intolerable to feel her friend pitying her.

"Miss Atkinson hasn't been well, poor thing. She had to go away for observation but she's back."

"What was it, rheumatism?"

"They call it arthritis now, she's got a stick."

"They'll be glad at Bampton's, she kept their accounts." The conversation wandered on in a disjointed way, never leaving the familiar lanes and cottages that were the whole of their life. "I never drank such a good tea as you make, Mabel."

"It's the water, we have the well, you know."

They sat and looked at each other, awkward in each other's presence for the first time in twenty years. "Ask your Mr. Robinson what to do when he gets home this evening. He was in business, wasn't he?"

"And he's going to mind it too. He wanted to settle in Trelawney."

"He wasn't born here, he can find some place else, but he ought to know what to do. It's always a question of getting the right person to speak for you." Lilian clung too much to that cottage, too much for her own good, Mabel had often said. "Now for myself," she leaned over to pour out the second cup of tea, "I shouldn't mind if they took this place tomorrow provided they gave me the right price for it."

THE CATCH LAY in the bottom of the boat. Two gulls above them seemed to fly as one. The overall pattern of the sea was the same yet every yard was a slightly different blue or moved in another way. A tangle of gold weed drifted by, almost but not quite on the surface of the water. "To think I have to leave tomorrow," Alex grumbled.

"Get stranded on an island," Robinson suggested lazily, he was wondering as he had often done before, why his friend had never mentioned the type of work he did during the year? It could not be that there was anything secret about it but rather that he wanted to forget it.

"Much too cold and uncomfortable at night."

Up to this very summer, Robinson remembered that he had had to go through the moods of the last day's fishing or the final walk. "Didn't you say you got a weekend in October? It's too late for boating then but the moors will be lovely. Come down as my guest."

"Somehow," Alex bent forward to coil a line that had come unwound, "I suspect there will be no holidays this autumn."

"Why ever not?" They were rocking on the waves as if only the continuous, gliding motion could break their peace. The sun was still warm enough to glow on their legs. They would land in good time to have supper and then watch it set over the hills.

"I don't like the possibility of a General Strike. I think your Green Coats of this morning are mixed up with it."

"Surely nobody sane could take those people seriously?"

"Are you sure that any of us is sane?" One of those superior and irritating smiles that sometimes put him out of temper with Alex, flashed for a moment across his friend's face. "That's the trouble. People are apathetic until it becomes too late. The Movement appeals to the residue of the barbarian in man that the intellectuals despise but have never tried to divert into channels where it would not be harmful."

"I'm not an intellectual," Robinson began to pull in his line, "we've argued this before and you know I agree with you. Besides, it's partly overpopulation."

"And one day Nature will send another Black Death to adjust the proportions."

"Stop being gloomy, Alex, and let us enjoy the evening. This has been one of the most perfect days I have ever had." He was aware of his selfishness before the words were out of his mouth, his friend was going back to the fogs and sleet and difficulties of a city winter while he would be able to walk to the headland and watch the gales sweeping in from the south west and blowing foam almost as high as the cliffs. "Do you know," he added inconsequentially, "I wish I could step ashore and die with this moment as my memory of earth."

Alex looked at him for a moment as if his eyes had turned into two piercing searchlights, "I wonder if you would say that if it happened?"

"I do not want a 'straw death,'" he answered lightly. It was the only dark thought beneath his present contentment. He could not stop the years from sliding on and there would come a time when he was too feeble to walk on the moors or step into Bill's boat. "I felt just the same when I was young but there was the sense then of things that I had to do. Afterwards, as with all of us, the development I felt bursting in me, grew a little and stopped."

It had been an endless waiting for a single moment but now, as if he was suddenly able to read a text in a previously unknown language, everything seemed clear.

The eternal hill and valley pattern repeated itself on the waves, a fisherman raised his hand in greeting under a brown, triangular sail and Bill steered the boat towards the entrance to the harbor. "I have a feeling that I shall never have another day like this myself," Alex admitted, "but perhaps things have to end or we should not love them."

"This is getting too complex," he felt the sudden fatigue that always came when moments were too near to perfection. He grasped the rope, they ran up the steps and Mrs. Blunt came forward. "Oh, Mr. Robinson, a dreadful thing has happened, I've been watching and waiting for you two gentlemen to arrive."

"THAT IS ALL there is to tell you," Lilian's wet handkerchief had made a stain on her pale blue frock. "The Carters, up the road, have got to move as well."

"It's monstrous," the face of Alex had gone purple with anger under his sunburn, "let me look at that form again."

"People like us have no rights any longer. Those Government officials never care."

"There are laws."

"Are you sure?" Robinson was sitting exactly opposite the china dog and was looking at it almost with affection. If only they had not let themselves flow into the perfection of that day on the water; that had been the flaw, the feeling had been so submerged as to be almost imperceptible, he ought not to have spoken of happiness.

"I wish I were younger," Lilian tilted back in her chair as she had always been scolded for doing as a child, "I would emigrate."

"I have sometimes felt that way myself," Alex put down the form, "here we are only links in an assembly line, not knowing how we began nor where we are going to end. Which country would you have chosen, Mrs. Blunt?"

"Well, a lot of my friends went to America and some went to New Zealand but I had a fancy it might be just like it was here, the same problems in a different landscape. Not that I didn't almost join the Thatchers when I was nineteen and they did well but then I married Harry. Now I should like to go to a place they say is utterly different. I want to go to Avalon."

"Avalon?" Alex was so startled that he looked at her almost rudely. "It's very unfashionable these days."

"As if I care! It sounds, as I just said, different."

"Let us take some positive measures first, Mrs. Blunt, before we talk gloomily about emigration. You can't let them ride roughshod over you like this."

"I thought I would go into Carrick tomorrow and see the Town Clerk. He was very good to me, you remember, when I lost half the roof in that dreadful gale. There was a fund and he got twenty pounds towards my repairs. I am going to put everything in front of him and hear what he says. And then," she jumped up so abruptly that she almost upset the table, "if that odious man was right and they can really take my house from me, whatever you gentlemen may say, I'm going to emigrate. What's the good of paying my taxes and trying to be a good citizen if they can rob me of everything I value?"

There was a constrained, anxious silence as they stood beside the door. None of them was accustomed to showing their emotions. Robinson stared at a second photograph of Lilian's terrier, if she had to move, it was a good thing that the dog had died. The clock struck seven. "Lilian," it was the first time that he had ventured to use her name in the fifteen years that he had known her, "come and have supper with us at the Dragon. Don't give that brute the satisfaction of knowing you are moping here alone all evening."

ALEX STRODE OVER the moor, several paces ahead of his friend. His temerity was beginning to worry him. He had wired the office that he would be late returning to work and that meant a day less on his next holiday. All the same, he was determined to wait until Mrs. Blunt had returned from Carrick and they had discussed the matter again. There might be something that he could do for her in town, hand her case over perhaps to some society that specialized in such cases though his common sense told him that it was hopeless. It annoyed him, however, that the reward of his good deed was not an extra day's fishing but a fog.

How old the landscape was! They walked past knots of gorse, a rock like a hare's ear, the ash of some withered thrift. The mist lifted a little as they reached higher ground but autumn was in the air, the melancholy of a summer's end that no lifetime would repeat. All that mattered was experience and the lessons to be learned from it, yet where was the mercy if man failed?

"I'm afraid there is nothing we can do for Lilian," Robinson brushed against a clump of high grass and felt the moisture brush off on his raincoat.

"Absolutely nothing."

"I think I shall emigrate as well."

"Why? You like it here and there are plenty of other villages."

"But always the fear of a road. No, I was happy at the cottage but I feel Trelawney leaving me, slipping away like the bark from a tree. We are growing poorer, even in our minds, and wherever I look I see darkness." Perhaps if he had always lived in the village he would have been caught up in its jealousies and rivalries but it had been an outpost to him where the link between a savage with a flint knife (how easily one might be hiding now at the back of that gray boulder) and the cells of his own body had seemed to run in an uninterrupted line. The past spun through his head like a roll of film but he could not pierce the blank wall of the future.

"Each man's experience marks him according to his generation," Alex went on as if he had never broken off the conversation five minutes earlier, "only we seem to have been born at a moment when the continuity has broken."

"The question is, how can we help Lilian?"

"I wonder what made her think of Avalon? I'm surprised she has ever heard of it."

"The sailors used to talk about it when I came here as a boy. There was a story that nobody who landed there ever returned."

"It's extraordinary that sailors should be so romantic when they have to lead a continuously practical life if they are to survive. There are very great landing difficulties but the climate is excellent. The inhabitants probably want to stay where they are."

"Perhaps if Lilian insists on leaving, we can persuade her to go somewhere nearer. I wish she would stay inside the country at least and not dash off where she has no friends."

"Isn't that the advice I have been giving you?"

A plant of the deep purple heather that was a feature of the place had forced its roots into a cleft between two stones. A wind was rising and blowing away the last remnants of the fog. "There's my answer," Robinson pointed to two men who were setting up a theodolite on the most ancient part of the moor, "the road is going to run as far as the headland."

THEY STOOD AMONG the crowd at the bus stop, waiting for Lilian to arrive. Robinson was too restless to keep still; he walked up and down the narrow pavement, marveling at his friend's patience. He was not lonely, he felt the globe revolving round him, the children with their ice cream cones, a woman

rushing into a shop before it closed for something she had forgotten, a man passing with a coil of rope from the harbor. It
was simply a feeling that the events of the last two days, though
not from his own volition, had detached him from the world.
The things that his mind needed in order that it could live were
being abolished by the new pattern being pressed upon the
national life. "Bus must be late," he said, stopping in front of
Alex who answered him with a teasing grin. "Buses are late,
shops shut at odd times, soon there are going to be no trains,
everything is upside down and…" he repeated the favorite expression, "there's nothing that we can do about it."

An old man got up from the solitary bench. It was a
signal. "He's so deaf he never hears the lifeboat alarm, how
does he know the bus is coming?"

Alex shrugged his shoulders, "Wait here, she will see us
more easily if we don't get mixed up with the crowd."

Lilian was almost the first to get out, her second best
shopping bag bursting with parcels and a rent in her shabby,
brown handbag. "It was no use," she said but this time without tears, "Mr. Brown was as nice as nice but there's nothing he can do to help me. I think he's frightened that his own
place may be next. There are forty of us on the first list and
all we can fight about is compensation. He gave me the name
of a lawyer. It's that Mr. Andrews from the Cliff who comes
here sometimes to fish. 'I wish I could help you, Mrs. Blunt,'
he said because I had taken the deed with me and I went to

him at once with my problem. 'You can sometimes get round the law but you can't fight the Requisition people.' I've left everything in his hands."

"When do you have to quit?" Alex was always practical.

"Six months is the limit and it may be earlier. This stage of the road will be the one they start first."

"Oh, Lilian!" Robinson could not think of anything comforting to say, at such a moment all he could feel was rage.

"It's hard on you as well, Mr. Robinson. I know you liked Rose Cottage. But I think Mrs. Brentford might take you in."

"I shall not stay here."

"What are you going to do, Mrs. Blunt?" Alex asked gently.

"Emigrate to Avalon if they will have me."

"I think you would miss your own country, you know."

"Of course I shall miss my country but when an odious little man walks in with hardly a by your leave, and turns you out of the house you've lived in all your life, what can it mean to you any longer? A country ought to be the same as a home. If I were younger there are other places where I might go but as it is, I had better try Avalon. They are not so fussy there about age."

Standing there, with her shopping bag clasped like a turkey under her arm, she looked so implacable that Alex had to smile. The kiosk was deserted, the papers had been sold and the postcards moved inside for the night, even the bus had been driven back to the garage.

"I shall have to make some inquiries," Robinson thought with dismay of the long, dreary journey that he had not expected to take again for at least another year, "suppose I go back with you tomorrow, Alex?"

"Who told you about Avalon, Mrs. Blunt?" Alex asked instead of replying to the question.

"A sailor my father knew used to talk to us about it. I thought even then that if I ever traveled, I should like to go there."

"I wonder where I can make inquiries?" It was terrifying how much of the assurance of his city life had left him. After all, Robinson felt in his pocket for his notebook, he had only been four months in Trelawney and now it was an effort to remember the numbers of his usual buses, "Do you think it would help if I rang up Information?"

Alex was staring down the alley that led to the shore. There was just a glimpse to be seen of rough waves racing like little puppies between the old houses and the sheds. He seemed to be thinking about something and Lilian moved her bag to the other arm. There was an awkward pause with nobody knowing what to do. Then Alex turned and looked at them again and for the first time they saw him hesitate. "No, not Information, if you have really made up your minds I might be able to help you. You see, I work at their consulate myself."

TWO

WAVE AFTER WAVE thundered into the cove to dissolve in rainbows above the rocks. They were full of the terror of death, of the return to the caldron of the sagas, where what was finished was swept away and new patterns formed from the atoms. On his way to the headland Robinson had been so conscious that this was his final walk that he had hardly noticed earth or sky; now the scene was beginning to blur into his habitual stroll before supper. Age was rather an exhaustion of the emotions than a physical fatigue and memories were troubling him more at that moment than leaving Trelawney the next morning.

A tuft of dead thrift was blowing in the wind but the rocks above him formed a shelter. He had expected to end his days in the village, also protected from storms, but fate had decided otherwise. Mankind was telling itself the same story over again. It could not bear its hidden desires to be uncovered and if one came to the surface, some repressive movement rose to fight it. To be free was to be responsible but the people who were driving Lilian and himself into exile, dreaded personal decisions more than slavery. How ironical life was! They now possessed a knowledge of the inner workings of the mind no other centuries had known and it was precisely against such understanding that the revolution was directed. Anything but wisdom was the slogan they would chalk up on the walls. Search, except within narrow limits, was a new word for sin.

"Yes," Alex had said when Robinson had seen him off at the station, "you had both better leave although I can't do much about the visa, the consul's very sticky. I wish Lilian were ten years younger."

"She won't survive parting with Rose Cottage if she has to stay here."

"Well, try anyhow, here's a letter of introduction and a card with the address but don't say a word in the village. The less your 'evasion' plans are known," and he had laughed, "the greater your chance of success."

A spray of withered bracken hung over a stone as if it were some strange red skeleton, a fish perhaps, left there to dry. Beside it, the golden pods of newly opened gorse were turning September back to March. The sea was a darker blue than usual, the sky was dark, but a single patch of sunlight fell across the smooth, ribbed pattern of the waves. How like life, he thought, a golden day but brief, then the uniform grayness of the months.

It was time to return or Lilian would fuss about the supper getting cold. He had offered to take her to the Dragon but she had refused, "Mabel is coming to see me afterwards. I'd rather say good-by to her at the cottage while it is still my own than in all of a turmoil at the station."

He looked just once more at the headland and thought he saw islands tracing themselves in the foam.

THE FIRST PART of the journey was through a countryside almost as familiar to them both as Trelawney itself. The heather was beginning to darken on the moors but here and there they caught sight of patches that were still the faded rose of the thrift. They passed through several villages that they knew, where in spite of the apparent sleepiness of the whitewashed cottages, a busy life was going on in the kitchens and gardens. Scones were being baked, old men were tying pea sticks into bundles and once they saw a broken fish basket half full of pebbles on a strip of grass. The scene was as much a part of them as their own bodies. It occurred to Robinson suddenly that he would miss the autumn smells in the fields. October had a different scent from July; summer was trampled bedstraw and green honey, autumn was crushed bracken and blackberries. "Suppose we don't like Avalon when we get there?" he whispered so as not to disturb the old man drowsing in the opposite seat.

"It's too late to think about that now," Lilian had the expression of "it's washing day and out you go" on her face. "Have you got that card that Mr. Magnus gave you?"

"Of course," he took it out of his pocket. It was a plain piece of cardboard with an address on it in his friend's bold, sprawling handwriting. "Where did you first hear about Avalon yourself?"

"I told you, from a sailor."

"Did he get there?"

"Yes, I think so because he never came back. The journey's difficult from what he said."

"Oh, that was in the old days when you had to go by sea. It's much easier, Alex told me, by air."

"You know, I can't imagine it at all."

People would call them crazy to leave for a new country at their age rather than give up "a bit of independence." There were moments when Robinson was tempted to agree with them. It was, however, almost a moral question. If an individual's right to a place of his own were not respected, it was the first link in a chain that would ultimately lead to the elimination of the unwanted by any group that happened to be in power. "We have to make a stand, I suppose," he said with such a question in his voice that Lilian looked at him in amazement. "If you have any regrets about coming, Mr. Robinson, I am quite capable of making my journey alone."

"No, it was the injustice that was troubling me, I'm as anxious to leave as you are." He did not add, "If we can get the visa," in spite of the warning that it would be difficult. "It's not my department," Alex had said, "and I've never known how they make up the lists but they seldom give out more than a dozen a year."

The fields gave way to rows of little houses, the spire of a church, a billboard and the chimney of a factory came into view beyond a winding street, the train slowed down and they stopped at Carrick station, their market town and a junction where they had to stop for half an hour.

"This is the worst moment of the journey, waiting for the express and wondering if we'll get seats." The train was usually full by the time that it reached Carrick and there were two methods of approach. The first was to get in casually and hope for the best and the second was for the most aggressive member of the party to spring like a racer into the corridor, leaving the others to follow with the luggage. Robinson glanced at the pile at their feet. Alex had warned them that they would have to travel light and it had been easier for him than for Lilian. He had sold or given away many of his possessions before going down to Rose Cottage. After he had handed a bundle of old fishing clothes to Bill and left a box of books with Mabel Ashford until he could send her directions what to do with them, the rest of his things had gone easily into a suitcase and his overnight canvas bag, a relic of his former business flights. Lilian had been ruthless, she had disposed of many of her belongings and left the rest in Mabel's care but she had arrived at the station with three overstuffed bags and a flat, plastic case. "I wish you had let me get you something solid," he said, looking at the bucket-shaped receptacle with a rope handle, the black-and-white checked picnic bag with a thermos sticking out of the top and a sort of schoolgirl satchel that she usually carried suspended from her shoulder.

"Waste of money," her face seemed rounder and firmer than usual, "these are light, I can carry them myself if we can't get a porter and if I have to put one down for a moment, it's much less likely to be stolen than some expensive bit of luggage." She looked with scorn at his own rather battered case.

There was a whistle, a confusion of sounds from the loudspeaker that nobody could have separated into words, the coaches drew up along the platform, Lilian sprang into the train and while Robinson was still pushing through the crowd with as much of the baggage as he could carry, her head popped out of the window and she shouted, "I've got two seats."

"Splendid," he dropped the first load and rushed back for the rest. One was in the corner and the other was a middle but next to it. "We'll take turns," Lilian declared, it was the accepted practice since he had been a boy, and the only difference that the years had made to the trip was that the carriages were much, much dirtier. "The filth!" Lilian took the advertisement page out of the newspaper that she had just bought and spread it over the cushion, "You would have thought with the price they charge now for tickets, they could afford a little soap and water."

There was a murmur of approval from three of their fellow travelers, two of them looked as if they might be sisters while the third was an older woman in a plain, brown dress with a straw hat perched on top of her head. The other corner was occupied by a man morosely reading his newspaper. "I don't believe they ever wash the carriages at all and it makes the end of the holiday even more dismal." The speaker smiled at Lilian and gave a little pat, as if to beat the dust from it, to the folds of her bright red dress covered with white flowers.

Robinson stowed their things away on the already overcrowded rack and stared out of the window, almost without noticing the landscape. Lilian checked her ticket and the women resumed a conversation that their entry had evidently interrupted.

"I love a cinema myself but I never seem to get to see a thing," the younger sister (if they were related), in a blue dress covered with white dots that had obviously been washed several times, lolled against the back of the seat.

"I never go to films, I'm much too busy."

"There seems so much more to do these days," the white flower in front of the older woman's hat bobbed forward like an overgrown peony.

"There are fewer deliveries. Where we live they never come round with the bread and as for help ..." she threw her hands out in a surprising gesture of despair.

"I enjoyed Porth. You can say what you like but I'd rather have a week there, it's so friendly and comfortable, than a fortnight like we had last year in one of those parties abroad." The straw hat caught against the seat and its owner took it off to put it on top of her coat in the rack.

"You went on a coach, didn't you, dear?"

"Yes, and I don't know where we stopped, I got so muddled."

"It was like old times at Porth. They left us out some cold ham for supper last Sunday, the sort you used to get with a real flavor to it, not this new preserved stuff."

"That's what makes me angry to have to go back today but everybody said we should never get through tomorrow. We should be due at the station just as the Demonstration started."

"What Demonstration?" Robinson asked anxiously. It was rude but they had been so busy since Alex had left that he had never looked at the news and Lilian had moved her television set immediately to Mabel's cottage.

"Haven't you heard?" they all began to talk at once, "the Movement is holding a big procession tomorrow."

"They talk of a General Strike."

"First thing in the morning I am going out to get enough food for several days."

"I am going up to the Demonstration, I want to see the speakers."

"You'll be lost in the crowd. Better watch it comfortably on T.V."

"I want to know what the Movement intends to do."

"Yes, I turn off the T.V. when it comes to the news, I can't stand anymore of their meaningless gabble about cooperation with a lot of foreigners. You don't even find it among your own neighbors, it's just grab, grab, grab."

"If my place was broken into while I was away, the old man next door wouldn't even bother to phone the police."

"It's the taxes. The Government itself has taught us to fiddle. You can't save, I try not to think about what will happen when I get old, we're far worse off than when I was a child."

"We need more discipline."

"Why?" The word escaped from Robinson's mouth and they all looked at him as if he had made an obscene remark but he could not let such a statement pass without protest.

"I suppose you approve of those teenagers cuddling each other and yelling," the woman in brown picked up her straw hat again as if it were unseemly for her head to be uncovered, "I think they ought to be thrashed."

"It's only one group among many and you won't get results that way." The age-old remedy of suppressing whatever the populace in power disliked, had never worked throughout history. Whenever an urge was repressed, it would break out somewhere else.

"And what would you do?" When she turned to look at him full face, he noticed the harshness of her mouth.

"Study the matter scientifically." The psychologists had put the tools into their hands but it would be generations before people accepted them.

"Oh, you're one of those people!" There was no mistaking the sneer in her voice.

"We need a group to bring some order back into public life," the man in the corner put his paper down for the first time, "but I doubt the capacity of these parading idiots even to govern themselves."

"My brother is a member and he's no idiot."

"There may be exceptions, madam, but wrecking our trade and upsetting our way of life are not going to help us out of our very grave difficulties."

There was an awkward silence. The man picked up his paper again. Lilian stared out of the window as if she had not listened to a word of the conversation. The majority of people unconsciously wanted the barbarians and in such a struggle, reason was not quick enough to defend itself and the barbarians usually won.

Robinson happened to look up that moment at a field. It was an ordinary meadow. A little stream ran through it, curving slightly to one side just before it reached a small clump of trees. He had noticed it year after year as a boy, it was a sign of the beginning of the holidays but, perhaps because of some repression or because he was sitting on the opposite side of the compartment, he had always missed it on his return home. Was it a sign, seeing it suddenly at this moment, that the Trelawney part of his life was dead? It was not a place that a photographer would have chosen for a picture; it was damp and without special beauty and he could not have explained to any other person why it seemed a symbol of his own land. It was only grass and water, with today an old brown pony standing in the distance beside a bank. The scene passed, telescoping with memories of his early days and the next flat pasture, it was apparently the same, had nothing to offer to his mind. "I shall be glad when we arrive," he murmured to Lilian, "there's such a lot to do tonight."

Actually he merely wanted to walk round some of the familiar streets because he had broken his links with the City on the day that he had left for Trelawney. It would be absurd to speak of Alex as secretive but they had seldom met except during the holidays and he did not want his friend to think that he was pressing him about the visa. He had always felt that under the surface Alex led a different life to his own. This was the moment when he would miss his apartment but he was taking Lilian to a small but fairly central hotel where his aunt had stayed on her annual visit to see him, until her death a couple of years before his retirement.

It was a curious fact but the conversation of his fellow travelers had counteracted the misgivings that he had felt and hidden from Lilian, about his own emigration. It was also a fact (sometimes he had doubted it) that they would build the road and obliterate the moor. The Movement would succeed, largely because of apathy, and the sooner he could get away the better.

Nobody spoke, several of them dozed, the minutes went by, slowly at first and then quickly, until in the late afternoon they left the countryside behind, street succeeded street, they drew up along a long, grimy platform and raced to join the queue that waited for the inevitably infrequent taxis.

To FEEL SO strange! He had been absent for only a few months yet Robinson felt as if he were revisiting a city that he had seen in his youth and where everything seemed half remembered. It was less that the streets had altered although they had passed several new buildings on their way from the station, but here a detail was perfectly familiar and then there was a forlorn, frightening sensation as if he were on a stretch of water, floating away from anything that he had ever known.

"Good evening, Miss Webb, have you many guests?" The secretary had made quite a friend of his aunt and he had always been grateful to her for her kindness to the old lady.

"We're full, though I can't think where some of the poor dears get the money from. A last fling, I suppose. What do you think of the situation, Mr. Robinson?" She slapped some papers that she was sorting back into a drawer.

"Not much, I'm afraid, but sometimes if people get power, they change when they realize the difficulties. I must say it was quieter in Trelawney but Mrs. Blunt and I have both business in town."

"I'm glad I have the chance of saying good-by to you. You won't find me here on your next visit."

"You're not leaving?" Miss Webb in her smart but slightly old-fashioned black dress with the fresh white collar that she clipped onto it every morning, seemed as much a part of the hotel as the wooden desk with the pigeonholes for letters at the side.

"I'm not only leaving, but I'm going overseas. Now I'm going to surprise you. I've got a visa for America."

"Miss Webb!" He was truly and utterly astonished. He had never credited her with a life at all outside the hotel.

"I've been restless for quite a long while, no, I suppose I'd better be frank and call it frightened. When they had those riots in June, I thought what am I doing, staying on here? The hotel will close if things go on like this or even be taken over. So I wrote my sister, you didn't know I had a sister in America, did you?" Robinson shook his head. "Well, it took a bit of time to get the papers but she helped me and I'm flying there next month."

"I do hope you'll be happy there."

"I was a bit nervous, you know, being fifty, but having a sister helped a lot."

The same migratory urge seemed to be going through a whole group; was there a yet undiscovered nerve that sounded an alarm when a world change happened? "I think you are very wise, you must give me your address tomorrow," he was about to tell her of their own plans when he remembered the warning not to speak of Avalon. "Oh, Mr. Robinson," Lilian came up at that moment almost as if it had been planned, "I'm dying for a cup of tea, do you think it's too late to get one?"

He led her into the lounge that was reasonably crowded, considering that the summer holidays were not yet over. "We stop serving tea at five," the waitress said, picking up a tray from the next table.

"We've just arrived after a very long journey," he had little hope that this would soften the woman's heart, "and by your clock it is still six minutes to the hour."

"I'll see what I can do, sir, but they shut the kitchen."

"Mr. Carter would never have done a thing like that at the Dragon. I've known him cook a meal for a traveler with his own hands. After all, we left at seven and except for that cup of coffee at the station, we've hardly had a thing since. I know I made the sandwiches myself but I couldn't fancy eating them in that filthy carriage."

The furniture had been new and even fashionable thirty years before but the colors had faded from extensive cleaning so that it was hard to say whether the curtains were blue or green. He suspected that a spring in his armchair was broken; it was lopsided and almost touching the ground. His neighbor stared at him and he stared back, fascinated by the cap she was wearing on the back of her head. It was made apparently of white linoleum with an edging of coral beads. "She's been through it a bit," she declared and her two companions, one of them was sitting beside her on the sofa and the other bolt upright on a chair, both nodded.

"But she's got the most awfully attractive little house in the mews behind the fish shop."

"I'm afraid she's quite a lass, you know, but she gets away with it."

"And it's not good for her."

"The truth is, she's a very lonely little lady."

"I thought she was sweet myself." The thin woman, the one that was as erect as an old-fashioned schoolmistress, tried loyally to defend the girl. She had obviously gone through life in an effort to please everybody. A pair of white gloves, apparently unworn, lay on her lap. She had carried them, no doubt, on special occasions during half a dozen seasons.

"I wish I had not forgotten my tape measure." The linoleum cap bobbed as its owner made the wildly inappropriate remark.

"Do you suppose she really wants one?" Lilian whispered.

"Don't ask, unless you want them to talk to you all evening."

Fortunately the waitress arrived that moment with a tray. "Cook let me have this although they were just closing down." She waited hopefully for the extra tip.

A revolution was in being outside the windows and there his neighbors were, arguing over some neighbor's daughter who was trying to break from the fold, without the slightest apprehension that the morrow might bring them poverty, imprisonment or even death. He wondered quite seriously if some corner could not be found for them, a reserve not for animals but for this world that was the one before his own, where they could pass quietly into oblivion?

Lilian looked very tired and devoted herself in silence to her tea. He hoped it was not going to be too much of a strain for her in the morning. The fear in his own mind was worse than any toothache he had ever suffered. Alex was able to blot the future out of his head, but Robinson could not lose himself in the moment; his thoughts ranged forwards and back, ending always with the picture of those girls on the quay, marching like a long green caterpillar with many legs and one rudimentary brain, after their leader. He wanted to walk till he was exhausted and then come back and sleep but he knew that it would be unsafe to be out after dark. "There's nothing I hate as much as patience," he said, handing Lilian the plate of bread and butter, "I feel tonight I should like to smash some windows."

"Do you really, Mr. Robinson," Lilian poured herself a third cup of tea, "and you know, I always thought you were so sensible."

THREE

Please walk in without knocking

The notice was simply a bit of cardboard fastened to the door by a couple of tacks. One corner had buckled over and there was an errand boy's greasy thumb print at the bottom. A porter was stooping over a newspaper, his elbows on a battered, ink stained table, as Lilian and Robinson entered.

"We have appointments," Robinson said, holding out the cards. The porter took them unwillingly, checked them against a list at his side and flipped them into a wastepaper basket. "Waiting room's on the left," he grumbled and returned to the sports page without another word.

Robinson hesitated. He had an impulse to stoop down and rescue the card that Alex had given him and that he had treasured so carefully. It had become for him, at least, an emblem of security. "To the left," the porter repeated impatiently, his finger on a list of fixtures. Lilian took her lodger by the arm but as they tramped along the uncarpeted corridor, Robinson wondered why the consulate of even so small a country was left in such a condition. Yet the house must have been a comfortable place in its time. There was the carving of a dolphin over the empty fireplace inside the waiting room and a trace of blue paint visible under the dirty white ceiling. One applicant was already there, a boy smoking some cheap, strong cigarette. He occupied the first of a row of chairs that looked as if they had been bought at auction after the closure of a railway station.

Lilian sat down in the second one, swung her shopping bag into her lap and the handle broke. "Now wouldn't that happen just at the consulate!" she began to laugh, "Still it would have been worse if it had happened on the bus." The boy turned his head away in obvious disgust and Robinson knew what he was thinking. Why do old women come up on an excursion train from heaven knows where and then ask for a visa to Avalon?

"Did you drop anything?" Robinson looked at the floor. It had been recently washed but was covered with panes of chocolate colored linoleum that would have depressed a color-blind dog.

"No, it was just the strap. I could mend it if I had a bit of cord."

"When I was a child, an old man told me never to go out without sixpence and a bit of twine in my pocket."

"Don't give your age away. Sixpence used to be the price of a bed and now it will hardly pay a bus fare. Still it was a good idea."

Robinson felt in his pockets, not very hopefully, to end with a shout of triumph. In a corner of one lining he discovered a foreign coin and a bit of the blue and white twine they put round some hastily bought gift at an airport. "It's not very long," he said doubtfully.

"I think I can manage." Lilian began to whip it round the break when the door opened and a girl said, "First, please." She was in the usual uniform of a secretary's light blouse and dark skirt and from her voice, not from Avalon, but one of the myriad, hired workers who hurried out to the bus queues at five o'clock. The boy jumped up, almost knocking his chair over in his impatience, he stubbed his cigarette out on the clean if dismal floor and disappeared into the adjoining room. "Why was he in such a hurry?" Lilian whispered. "Nobody wanted to take his turn away from him."

Robinson understood, only too well. He had begun to shake with anxiety himself. "I wonder how long it will be before we are called?"

"Would you like to go first? You have always lots to do." Lilian tied a final knot and held the mended bag up for him to admire. It was a roomy, checked affair with surprisingly little inside it. "You know, I would sit here willingly till the afternoon. They are sure to turn me down because of my age and then I shall lose even hope. Alex warned us that they were difficult about visas, especially these last years. He said they used not to be so strict." She smiled at Robinson forlornly and he realized abruptly that beneath her bustle and common sense, she had never had more than a "perhaps it might happen" from life.

"I would rather know the worst quickly," but he wondered if this was really true? "I'll wait my turn. Have you ever known anyone try for a visa before? I wonder what they ask you?"

"I have no idea. Yet ever since Alex helped us, I haven't been so happy since I was a child. I stopped worrying about whether I had enough to pay the electricity bill and my fare and sat out on the cliffs when I ought to have been packing. The waves rolled over the sand just as if they were cockle shells and somehow I felt that everything would be all right."

"You'll get the visa," Robinson said instinctively although he knew no more about it than she did.

"I'm afraid not, but I had the few days."

Robinson smiled at her, yes, he thought, staring at the blue squares on her bag, what was her future but arthritis, a lonely room after Rose Cottage had been bulldozed, an eventual old people's home. Yet she was taking her day, something that he could never do, and he admired her for it. A door slammed. They turned expectantly and Lilian muttered, "Oh, what shall I do in the train tomorrow when I know I have been rejected?" He looked the other way in consternation because he was afraid that she was going to cry. "They can't refuse us all," he mumbled and the girl put her head round the door again and called out, "Next, please."

It was stupid. He had brought nothing to read and here he was, alone in the room, too impatient to sit still and yet afraid of losing his turn if he got up from his chair. Did he really want the visa? The endless waiting seemed a symbol of his life, of the years when fate or duty had held him prisoner, never free from the sensation that if he had had liberty he would have expanded instead of feeling himself perpetually contract; he could even have come to some sort of achievement although what this might have been he could not guess. Was even Avalon worth this squalid moment of anxiety in a despoiled and hideous room?

How ugly the linoleum was! Yet even if he had been sitting on the headland above a sea so smooth that it would have been hard to imagine either shipwreck or gale, would he have noticed it any more than these slabs and lines while he wondered and worried about his interview? What were "they" going to ask him? What tiny incident from his past would rise suddenly to condemn him?

"Next, please." Robinson jumped up as quickly as the others when the secretary opened the door. They had not kept Lilian long. He looked round at the empty row of chairs and then everything went out of his head except an impulse, was it tidiness, that made him stoop and pick up the knot of string that had fallen beside his feet.

49

THE OFFICE THAT he entered was as unlike the waiting room as possible. The walls had recently been distempered and there was a mixed blue linoleum on the floor that was, if ordinary, at least a neutral background. The secretary motioned him to take a seat in front of her and as he sat down, he noticed a sign on the desk with her name, Sheila Willis. She had her back to the window and he wondered if she ever turned round to look at the green leaves of a plane tree that grew in the neighboring square?

"I suppose you want me to fill up a form?"

"I must ask you a few questions but we pride ourselves on having streamlined the procedure." It seemed to him as he looked at her, and he was naturally curious about the people whom the Avalon consulate employed, that she was two different persons, not in the usual sense of a split personality but because she had drawn an opaque sheath over what she actually was. The girl in front of him was like a thousand other women who listened to a customer's complaints or typed out lists but at five she would emerge with a serious and puzzled face, ready to go to language classes twice a week to prepare herself for her next holiday or to take long walks and puzzle herself about the meaning of life in the country on Sundays. He could see her now in a windbreaker and red, woolen cap.

"I am going to take your answers directly on the machine. At least I can read my own typing, it's not a computer."

"Computers are unreliable. I was charged the other day for twelve cabbages and a sack of potatoes when I had ordered three bath towels."

"I suppose we shall learn how to use them in time," her smile changed almost at once to a look of brisk efficiency, "and now, may I have your name, date of birth and nationality?"

"In triplicate as usual?"

"You wouldn't take us seriously if I made a single copy."

"I should expect you then to read it." How many consulates in how many cities contained his life story? It was perhaps a consolation to know that they were filed away and never read. Governments were inquisitive but then, at root, of a total indifference, as the French would say. He gave the details although it was with a feeling of disappointment. It was stupid of him, but he had expected the Avalon procedure to be different.

"The names of both parents and their dates. Are they alive?"

"No." It was almost a hundred years since they had been born and as he gave the cold, bare particulars of their births and deaths, he realized, and it was with shock, that they had walked and driven across a free and flowing countryside and that Trelawney even today would seem as strange to them as the moon.

"Other near relatives?"

"None."

"Profession?" Was he sure that what he was answering was true? He mumbled and had to repeat himself.

"There's only one question more," Miss Willis continued brightly as if he must be very tired, "what is your motive for requesting the visa?"

How could he answer that on any official form? What would it mean to say that he was as ill at ease with the new-comers who had invaded his village as a fish was out of the sea? "Exploration," he muttered, it was the first word that came into his head.

"You have a letter from your sponsor and an affidavit from your bank?"

He nodded, he was sure that both were insufficient but he took them out of his wallet.

"And your vaccination and anti-typhoid certificates?"

"Here."

"No, don't give them to me, you will need them when you see Mr. Lawson." She ripped the questionnaire out of the typewriter and handed him the top copy. "You can't go in yet, he has not finished with the previous applicant but it won't be more than a minute or so." She glanced over her shoulder at the plane tree, setting that query at rest, and asked after a moment of rather awkward silence, "Do you travel a great deal, Mr. Robinson?"

"Whenever I can but I haven't been away now for some time."

"I went to Italy last summer. People said I should feel the heat but I thought it was lovely and my friend and I used to sit and have coffee in the square and watch the people go by. I wished it would never end." A yellow light blinked on her desk, it was evidently a signal. "You can go in now, you see, we did not keep you very long, Mr. Lawson is ready for you."

The next room was smaller. It was furnished exactly like Sheila's office except that there was a carpet on the floor. Perhaps the waiting room was made deliberately unattractive to frighten merely inquisitive callers away?

"Sit down, please," Mr. Lawson said pleasantly and Robinson felt that he had seen the face before. On an airport perhaps or in some hotel?

"It's a sunny day for a change." The phrase, because it was commonplace, startled him. Had those eyes, with so much experience and authority behind them, already looked at Avalon?

"The climate in general seems to be altering. It's getting colder and wetter."

"Oh, these things go in cycles." He took the papers Robinson handed to him and spread them on his desk. "You want a visa?" he inquired.

It was on the tip of his tongue to say, "Why should I have asked for an appointment otherwise?" but he managed to control himself, these interviewers had more power than a sultan. "I have wanted to go to Avalon for years."

"I am afraid our quota is full up for some time."

"All the more reason for booking my place in the queue."

"Quite." He began to tick off the answers on the form. "Quite. Now let's see who your sponsor is." He opened the letter from Alex but, in spite of the brave words that he had used to console Lilian, Robinson knew that he had not got the shadow of a chance.

"You *know* Mr. Magnus?"

"We have spent our holidays together for some years."

"I often wondered if he had any friends."

"I don't know him well," he had the feeling that he must shield Alex at any cost, "it is easy to sit in a fishing boat for hours and never speak."

"Of course, it's a point in your favor that you do not claim any close acquaintanceship. But now, and be careful how you answer me, what is your real reason for wanting this visa?"

At that moment Robinson did not know or could not put into words what the inner side of his mind wanted to say. "Development," he suggested and knew at once it was the wrong expression. To him it meant growing but today it had become what they were doing to Trelawney, bulldozers razing cottages and machines cutting trees.

"You must be firmer about your motives."

"It is not that I am against the modern world. I should like to volunteer for the moon. But we do not use the knowledge that we have and I do not like what they are doing to the old. If a citizen has worked hard for fifty years, he deserves a little kindness."

"Changes are hard but they are a part of renewal. Nations grow, make mistakes, have their moments and then perish. Perhaps you are burdened with too many beliefs?"

"I never expect anything."

"Not even a visa to Avalon?"

"Not even that." He knew he was not going to get the permit and was reckless. "But I want to go to Avalon more than I have wanted anything in my life."

"It is hardly an answer that we commonly receive but it might prove acceptable. Now what does your bank say about you?"

He had never seen the Avalon currency and he was not even sure what the units were. Mr. Lawson's desk was polished, there was a bowl of roses at one side, and a sheet of white paper under the scattered forms. He had lost but he wondered what had happened to Lilian and the boy?

"Dear me, dear me, Mr. Robinson, the bulk of your income comes from your pension and that would not be payable in Avalon."

"How long will it be payable here and what is it worth? We have a runaway inflation already."

"That is true and we might be able to find a job for you if you were willing to work."

"I am willing to work."

Lawson clipped the papers together and Robinson wondered if it were a sign for him to leave? He clung in a sort of desperation to his chair.

"In ordinary times, Mr. Robinson, I doubt if I would have entered your name on our list but Mr. Magnus has given you a personal recommendation. There are a few points I have to check so I suggest that you come back and see me again at three. The exit is there…" He pointed to a side door opposite his desk and nodded pleasantly as a sign that the interview had ended. "Your hat!" he called as Robinson's fingers were already on the door handle. He had left it behind on a chair.

"The lady asked me to tell you that she was waiting for you at the teashop opposite."

Only Lilian would have had the temerity to ask a policeman to do her errands for her. It was strange to see one posted outside the consulate on a perfectly quiet street but it had to do, no doubt, with some question of diplomatic etiquette. He thanked the man and wished him a hearty good morning before crossing the road.

The tearoom had hidden itself discreetly between a private house and a greengrocer's shop. Lilian was sitting at a table by the window, watching the door.

"Well, what happened?" Robinson asked.

For answer, she handed him her passport, a little smugly, he thought, and pointed to a page. "Visa 8004, valid for entry within two weeks of date of issue." Robinson stared at it and read it a second time. "You got it? You actually got it? They told me the quota was full up."

"Oh, Mr. Robinson, don't say they turned you down."

"Not exactly." He did not want to tell her how little hope there was. "I am to go for another interview at three this afternoon."

"Oh, so am I, but it's to see about transportation. That's what Mr. Magnus does, isn't it?"

"I think so."

"I wonder if I shall see him? I should have waited at the door for you but I suppose it was the journey yesterday, I came over quite faint. The policeman was awfully kind, 'What you want, madam, is a good cup of tea, there's a nice place across the road.' So I came over here and sat down."

"He told me you were here." It had been a greater strain on Lilian than he imagined because he knew now that in spite of her apparent matter-of-factness she had been deeply afraid. "Have you ordered?" he asked.

"No, not yet."

It was characteristic of her to have waited for him. He looked round and a waitress came up to them, one of the thousands in such places all over the city, in a clean white apron, with a cloth over her arm and her thoughts a thousand leagues away.

"A pot of tea, please."

"Indian or China?"

"Indian, please."

She bustled away and Robinson looked at the passport again. It was hard to repress a feeling of envy. Lilian's problem was solved. "I told you you would get it," he said by way of consolation. "Do you know when you are going to leave?"

"I said I'd like to go as soon as possible. I hate hanging around once I've made up my mind." The waitress slapped a tray down on the table and Lilian leaned over and patted his wrist. "Don't worry, Mr. Robinson, you'll get one too, I'm sure you will. I have to have you to look after me."

Robinson shrugged his shoulders. The consul, what was his name, Lawson, hadn't liked him. The list probably was full, people were trying to get away, but whatever happened he would not return to Trelawney. "I wonder what he said to the boy who went in before us, he was as jumpy as we were."

"Oh, he slammed the door before the secretary had finished filling up my form. Shall I pour the tea out, Mr. Robinson? I can do with a cup, I assure you, it's the first time I've sat down comfortably since I got up this morning."

The street was empty and a late summer sun was shining on a window box of pink geraniums that ran the length of the window. He supposed the tearoom would add an extra amount to the bill because of the flowers. For a moment he saw quite vividly a mass of white petunias along a wooden balcony in a Continental village. Why should this scene, from an almost forgotten holiday of twenty years previously, come suddenly into his mind? It had been a passing glimpse on a day when nothing important had happened. There were times when memory was only a nuisance; to comfort themselves against loss, people exaggerated its power. "You've never been abroad, have you, Lilian?"

"Not unless you count the holiday I had with Florence in the north. I never wanted to emigrate but if my home goes, they are taking in a sense my country with it."

"There is nothing we can do."

"No, as Harry used to say, we have to take the rough with the smooth."

Perhaps it was anxiety but as he slowly finished his tea, it seemed to have little flavor and he refused a second cup. His mind seemed to be numb. Nobody had bothered to snip off the heavy stem of a geranium that had wilted and turned brown. There was a patch of new linoleum by the entrance that did not quite match the rest of the floor. "I'll bring you the check now if you don't mind" (and woe betide them if they did!), the waitress put the bill on the table beside his elbow. "We're closing at twelve today because of the Strike."

The same thought struck them both at the same moment. "Does that mean that the buses will stop running?"

"Most of them have stopped already," the waitress pocketed her tip and pranced away towards the back of the shop.

They stared at each other. Suppose after getting the visa there was no chance of reaching the airport? Somehow the perfectly ordinary tearoom transformed itself into a cell. "Mr. Robinson!" To Lilian's amazement, her companion darted out into the street. Then she saw that he had jumped onto the step of a passing taxi and was arguing with the driver. She swallowed the rest of her tea, after all they had paid a thieves' price for it because she had seen the bill, picked up her bag by the middle so as not to strain the hastily mended strap and followed him over to the cab.

"Lilian, I want you to go to the hotel and get the bags. I paid my bill this morning and my suitcase is with the porter. Keep the taxi and come back to this address at once," he handed her a scribble on a piece of paper. "It's a garage I know and I will try to get a car there to take us down to the plane."

"I can't wait for the lady if she has to pack."

"Everything's ready, it won't take me five minutes."

"I was going 'ome. We 'ave to be off the streets by one o'clock."

"But it's only a quarter to twelve and not ten minutes away. I'll make it worth your while."

The driver still hesitated but Lilian was already in the cab. "Don't forget my suitcase," Robinson yelled as they started down the road. He would never have time to fetch it. Then he turned briskly down a side street. Whatever Lawson thought of him or not, it was an inspiration. If Bert were still at the garage, he could persuade him to take them to the airport, he had given him a lot of work not only for himself but for his friends, while he had still been at the office.

FOUR

"Afternoon!" Lawson barely looked up from his desk. He had emptied a drawer and was sorting its contents into different piles. Occasionally he crumpled a paper up in his fist and tossed it into the wastepaper basket.

"Aft'noon." Alex swallowed the word. He looked ill at ease in his dark city suit. "Thought I was never going to get back here. The crowds are dreadful and half the buses have stopped running."

"Something's up. With Headquarters asking us to check old applications and new people coming in, we haven't been so busy for years."

"I couldn't trace either of the men on the list you gave me. In one case the house had been demolished and an office block built in its place and in the other the person had moved. I got an address but the landlady was very rude."

"I had two people in this morning with letters you had given them. What made you think they were suitable applicants for visas?"

"They need them as much as any of the others."

"The one, a Mrs. Blunt, seemed a sensible woman. The man was vague."

"Not in a boat, sir. I go most summers to Trelawney and I've known them for years." It was a slight exaggeration because he had hardly spoken to Lilian before the incident of the road but under present circumstances he felt it was justified.

"Holiday friends. But why did you send them to me today of all days?" Lawson tore a bundle of forms in two and added something, it looked like a blank sheet of paper, to a pile at his side.

"Because they wanted desperately to go to Avalon and I couldn't see why such a harmless wish shouldn't be granted. There's nothing but a miserable old age for them here."

"They will share the fate of thousands of others who will dislike the coming changes as much as they do, as much, in fact, as we shall ourselves."

"Why couldn't you have given them a visa? Why must this office be so difficult, so frustrating and so smug?"

"If you must prowl up and down like a hyena, try not to thump my desk. I carry out a policy, I don't initiate it."

"Perhaps Avalon itself is obsolete."

"I'd sack you on the spot if I thought you meant what you have just said but you haven't been yourself since you got back from your holiday. It's hard settling down. Just for your ears, I feel it sometimes myself on Monday mornings."

There was a knock on the door and Alex jumped. Miss Willis took any excuse to come in rather than use the house telephone on her desk. "Mr. Augier is here, sir, with letters."

"Here! Today! Send him in, will you?" Lawson swept the papers in front of him together and rammed them back into the empty drawer. "That's funny, the flight day is always a Thursday. Go and ask Miss Willis, while I see him, if the new address you got for the other man on your list was ever registered?"

A young man walked briskly up to the desk. Nobody could have mistaken his profession even if he had not been in an air pilot's uniform. His tanned face made his eyes seem even bluer than they were and his movements were more precise than a sailor's would have been. He handed a sealed envelope to Mr. Lawson.

"Well, Augier, what sort of trip did you have? We didn't expect you till next week."

"They told me, sir, it was urgent."

"Sit down, sit down, while I read my orders."

If he ever won his promotion, and Augier could not help glancing down at the rings on his cuffs, he would vote to cut the time that any official had to stay outside Avalon. Something happened to a man on foreign service; some people remained aggressively themselves but far too many took on mannerisms from the countries where they were stationed. Lawson, for instance, was pompous and behind his coldness, frightened. Why had he never protested about being left here seven years or at least asked to be transferred?

"They don't give a man much time," Lawson dropped his pencil nervously and stooped to pick it up. "I suppose you are aware of the contents of this document?"

"Can't say I am, sir." Was the consul an utter fool? Did he imagine that a simple pilot would be entrusted with information prepared in the Chancellery and sealed with the Great Seal?

"I am to shut the office immediately and evacuate the staff. They anticipate disorders."

"To diplomats, sir?"

"Oh, they put it more tactfully. I am recalled for consultations."

"Then if I may suggest it, sir, the sooner we leave for the airport the better. If I had not known the shortcut by the reservoir I should not have been here for another hour."

"What time is the return flight?"

"Not till eleven, sir, but we shall be safer at the airport."

Lawson looked at his watch. It was quarter to three. "I shall leave at five as soon as the office is closed," somehow his routine held him, "but I think you had better go back immediately. How many passengers will the plane hold?"

"Six, sir, but couldn't you manage to start a little earlier? There's chaos on the roads."

"We do have diplomatic plates."

He was right, Lawson had been here too long and had fitted himself so thoroughly into his environment that he had taken over many of its complacent characteristics. As if the mob would bother to read the letters! Still, it was not for him in his junior rank to reply. "Can I take anybody down in my car, sir?"

"No, thanks, we have some work to do here first. I will go to the office at the airport when we arrive."

"The girl at the desk will know where I am," he hesitated and then forgot his habitual caution, "please, sir, leave earlier if you can or you may find the roads are blocked."

Lawson waited till the pilot had shut the door before reopening the drawer of his desk. Even Augier would have been surprised at the correctness of his observations. The consul did not want to leave, the homesickness of his first year in the post had vanished so completely that he hardly remembered it and all that he felt now was that he was abandoning his colleagues and friends to disaster. His routine had been pleasantly full and he was still too young to have thought about retirement. He read the directions over again on the stiff, white sheet of paper, looked up at the clock and lifted the house telephone. "Ask Mr. Magnus to come to me, please, Miss Willis. We are going to be very busy."

"Well?" Alex shut the door carefully behind him.

"We've had it, Magnus, it's immediate evacuation to Avalon."

"When?"

"In precisely…" he looked up at the clock again, "two and a quarter hours."

"But they can't abandon all the people who have trusted in them here! They can't fling them like this to the… to the…"

"Not wolves, Magnus, that's terribly out of date. Let's say to a computer."

"They're decent people and they trusted in me and I trusted in Avalon."

"Foolish of you. Haven't you read the posters that the individual must be sacrificed for the common good?"

"I can't face Lilian and tell her there's no hope."

"As a matter of fact, I gave Mrs. Blunt a visa this morning. She seemed a capable woman, likely to make a good citizen and I told her to be here at three to fix up her transportation with you. There's no room in my car but if she gets off at once, it should be all right. Tell her the flight is at nine. Has Miss Willis found any address for the man where the house had been demolished?"

"No, only the address of the sponsor."

"Then tell her to wire the sponsor. He may know where the fellow is. There is a reason, you see, behind all our regulations that you dislike so much. If the applicants can get to the airport in time, I will give them the visas there. Your friend can go down with Mrs. Blunt if he likes and if one of the men does not turn up, he can have the vacant place."

"Lilian has the visa?" A suppressed love for Avalon flooded back into his head.

"I am not in the habit of making inaccurate statements. But now I must list what we have to do. It is quicker in the long run to jot things down on a scrap of paper. First, there's our seal and some things to be taken out of the safe..."

"And the Bank?"

"Fortunately I went there yesterday. I admit the thought of evacuation never crossed my mind but I feared that our account might be blocked. I left just enough to keep it going and the rest of the funds are here. You had better make a start on burning our papers, I suppose you'll have to use the dustbin in the backyard but see your friend when he comes at three and I must have a word with Miss Willis."

Sheila was thinking when the door opened that nothing unexpected ever happened to her. She knew the date of her holiday months ahead and even the Sunday weather forecasts were usually vague: "Light showers may occur during the afternoon" meant that she was usually burdened with a mackintosh even in June. Everything seemed gray and predictable except for sudden moments on her way to work in the morning or a weekend adventure of finding an early pit of bluebells under an oak, but these were quick flashes of happiness rather than a continuous whole.

"Miss Willis!"

"Yes, Mr. Lawson." Something had happened, she had seldom seen him look so anxious and tired.

"I'm afraid those manifestations we have been witnessing are serious this time."

"It was rather difficult getting here this morning but tomorrow I can start a little earlier…" If she were unpunctual they might find somebody who lived nearer to take her place.

"I have been ordered to close the office."

"Oh, Mr. Lawson!" It was a wail of despair.

"I can either give you your salary for three months as this is such a sudden decision or I have been told I may take the staff with me if they wish. Would you care to go with us?"

"To Avalon?"

"There are certain disadvantages. You would have to leave with me tonight and take only a bag but there would be work for you there and it's a friendly place, you would soon settle down."

A thousand thoughts rushed through Sheila's head, the holiday plans that would have to be abandoned, her new dress that would get dreadfully crushed in her canvas case, the break with everything she knew. Then she heard people shouting in the street outside. What would she do in a typists' pool and having to listen to lectures on a collectivism in which she did not believe? She wasn't qualified for this new world and she knew it.

"I can give you an hour to make up your mind."

"No, Mr. Lawson, I'll come and gladly." She had not really meant to say gladly but she made no attempt to correct herself.

"Very well, there are two things for you to do before we leave. Try every way you can to trace those two men who were waiting for their visas. As I told Mr. Magnus, if they still want them and can get to the airport by nine tonight I will see them there. Then burn all documents except the bills. I can deal with those while I am waiting for the plane."

"Very good, sir."

Sheila studied the paper that Alex had left on her desk. Owen, she could not remember the man at all but she looked him up in her folder of applications. There were only a few details. He had come to the office several months previously, he had been a pilot but was then working at an office in the City, he had not notified them of any change of address. His new one was in the country and she dialed Directory. She wondered if there would be anyone there to reply but a voice answered her as usual. She listened, there was so much to do, but eventually she was given a number and was able to dial Trunks.

She was waiting, itching with impatience at the delay, when there was a sharp knock at the door. Lilian entered, looking very different from the neat figure of that morning, with a bulging canvas bag slung over her shoulder and a winter coat on her arm. "I'm sorry but there's no porter in the hall and I thought I had better let you know I was here."

"You're early, I'm afraid Mr. Magnus is still busy."

"Oh, I knew I should have to wait but the streets are dreadful. I thought I was never going to get across the main road. Mr. Robinson stopped at the post office at the corner but he'll be with us in a minute, I don't mind sitting here at all, it's so quiet." It was not true because she was anxious about Robinson and though she had the visa, she wondered if even with a private car, they would manage to catch the plane?

"Are the roads completely blocked?" Sheila ought to have told Mrs. Blunt to go to the waiting room but at the moment she felt her presence reassuring. The thought that she was giving up everything to go with the consul was spinning round in her head. At least her opportunity had come but she could not help wondering about the people she knew, the nice couple in the country who rented her a room sometimes at Easter and never minded drying her wet clothes, a girl from the language class who waited with her for the same bus, and the old fellow at the kiosk where she bought her newspaper. What were they going to do when the rebels took over? "They won't help us workers," he had often said when she had exclaimed over a headline, "they're using people so a few agitators can get to the top."

The phone rang and she snatched up the receiver, wondering as she gave the consulate number if it would be the last call to come through to the office. "Can I speak to a Mr. Owen, please."

"Speaking." The voice sounded a little hoarse.

"This is the Avalon consulate. Your visa has just come through if you want to take it up."

"I do." The man showed no surprise that it was six months since he had heard from them nor that they had found his new address.

"As you may know, there are disturbances here, but a plane is going to Avalon tonight. If you can be at the airport by nine this evening, you can fly out with the consul. Remember, only fifteen kilos of baggage is permitted."

"Where shall I report?"

"At our desk in the main hall. Mr. Lawson will give you the visa there."

"Thanks." The receiver was slammed down and she judged that Mr. Owen was both decisive and in a hurry. She tapped at the consul's door. "I've traced one of the applicants, sir, and he will try to join us but I've had no luck with the other man as yet."

"I know you are doing your best but we must make every effort we can to reach him."

Sheila shut the door again just as Alex burst into her own room, a towel round his waist, his hands covered with thick, black dust, and a gray smear across his forehead. "Have you ever tried to burn a year's correspondence in a broken dustbin?"

"No, Mr. Magnus, and I don't want to either. Here's Mrs. Blunt to see you about her transportation."

"Sorry, Lilian, I didn't notice you in that corner. I hear you got the visa, where's Robinson?"

"At the post office. He'll be here any minute."

"And you want your ticket?"

"Please, Mr. Magnus." It seemed an arid statement but Lilian could think of nothing else to say. She knew from the manner in which Alex was acting that the disturbances were even worse than she had supposed. "Mr. Robinson has hired a car. He says it is the only chance of getting to the airport."

"And he's right. Now about your ticket."

"It just needs your signature," Sheila said, "I got it ready this morning."

It was while he was writing his name in the space provided for the purpose that Alex felt the force of his own fear. "Evacuate the staff." But he was a Temporary. Did Lawson mean to take him or not? Yes, he had once made that mistake, but it was years ago, in a moment of revulsion from change when he had been utterly exhausted, but they had never forgiven him. He longed to ask the consul at once but pride forbade him to say a word. He blotted the page and watched Sheila helplessly as she soaked the ink up with a pad. "Here you are, you must be there by nine and you pay the tax when you arrive." Then he knocked at Lawson's door, "Come for another load, sir," he imitated an office boy, oh, if only the man would say a word to settle his fate.

"You look a bit tattered," Lawson said with some amusement.

"Try burning documents in that rusty tin downstairs and see what happens."

"Well, this is your last load. I shall leave the other papers on the floor with a note and a bit extra for the charwoman, asking her to finish up tomorrow."

"Mrs. Blunt is here. I've given her her ticket but she is waiting for Mr. Robinson. He has managed to hire a taxi."

"An excellent idea. Sign a ticket for him on your way through but take it with you. If the other applicant doesn't turn up, he can have his place."

Lawson watched his colleague stagger out with a huge and awkward wastepaper basket in one hand and a roll of legal documents under his other arm. Poor Alex! He was as nervous as a chained dog that smelt fire but he had been so imperious and difficult at times that he would leave him now till Magnus was forced to ask about his own evacuation. "I've brought you a cup of tea, sir," Sheila actually came into the room without knocking, "it's early but we shall be busy later with last-minute things."

"That's thoughtful of you. Send Mr. Robinson in as soon as he arrives."

"He's waiting, sir."

"Send him in. I can drink my tea while I talk to him."

Robinson looked anxious but calm. He had a briefcase with him but otherwise his appearance was unchanged since the morning. "If you have no objection, sir, I have hired a car and I will take Mrs. Blunt to the airport."

"I was just going to suggest that myself. There are two applicants above you on our list. One is meeting us there but we have had some trouble tracing the other. If he doesn't turn up by nine, then I will give you the visa."

"Oh, thank you, sir, thank you very much."

"He may turn up so don't be too hopeful. I suggest you both get off as soon as possible. Wait for us at our office in the airport or if you want to have some food, let the girl there know where you are."

"Thank you, sir." It was a repetition but this was no moment for conversation. He rushed out and grasped Lilian's arm. "I may have a chance at the airport, it depends upon how many turn up. The consul says we are to leave at once. Here, let me take your bag."

"Going with us?" Sheila asked.

"If there's room. Tell Mr. Magnus we hope to see him later, come, Lilian, the sooner we leave the better."

Sheila listened to their footsteps clattering down the hall and hoped Mr. Robinson would get his place. She swallowed her tea slowly while she tore up the papers in her desk, surely Mr. Lawson couldn't mean her to destroy clean notepaper, and put the few bills into a big envelope. There was a whole

box of new pencils and she thrust these into her handbag.
You never knew when a pencil might not come in handy.

It was a moment for something stronger than tea, Lawson looked at even the clumsy brass inkstand with affection,
but the routine soothed him. He checked that the money, the
seal and his credentials were all in his briefcase. It had never
been so full for years. He picked up the letter that Augier
had brought him, to confirm for the third time that he was
carrying out his instructions. A flimsy sheet of paper was still
crumpled up inside the envelope. "Leave Mr. Magnus free to
make his choice but bring him with you if he wishes." Well,
that settled the matter, it was for Alex to choose. In a flood
of pleasure that he was absolved from responsibility, he swallowed his tea at a single gulp.

"I suppose I'm getting the knack!" Alex came in with another black smear across his chin, "The second lot was easier."

"It seems so useless. I've spent hours working on those
papers. Really, the stupidity of the human race is beyond understanding. You know," and Lawson looked round the room
from the legal books in the glass fronted case to the vase of
flowers on his desk, "I am really sorry to leave."

"Yes."

Lawson looked at his colleague without answering. He
would make him forget his pride and ask. Then it occurred
to him that they might have wanted him to "work out" (a
favorite phrase of theirs) his old habit of overmeticulous

scruples before admitting him to the full citizenship that he had earned. "Well, Magnus, what are you going to do? Have you decided to come with us?"

"I was not sure that Temporary was Staff. Is there room?"

"There are three of us, Miss Willis is coming as well, Mrs. Blunt, a fellow, Owen, and if we cannot trace the other applicant, your friend, Robinson, can take his place."

"Another cup of tea, Mr. Lawson?" Sheila came into the room with the tray.

"Why, I seem to have drunk my first one without noticing. Yes, please, Miss Willis, if there is any left. Is there any news about the second applicant?"

"I telephoned a wire to his sponsor explaining the situation. But it's somewhere right up in the north."

"Then get your personal things together and the bills. We are leaving in a quarter of an hour. I have a feeling that our diplomatic plates are not going to be much use to us this evening and we have got to go to our apartments." All glanced up at the clock. It was a quarter to four.

FIVE

THE SITUATION HAD completely altered during the half hour
that they had been at the consulate. The main street that was
less than three minutes away was jammed with people apparently unable to move. "Come, Lilian," Robinson took her
by the arm, "I know a short cut to the garage."

It was habit that kept them to the pavement because there
were neither cars nor cycles on the road. Fortunately they
were going in the opposite direction from the crowds. It was
the route that Robinson had taken hundreds of mornings
during his working life; sometimes an irrational feeling of
freedom had come to him when he had smelt salt in the air
on a windy day, at other times he had pressed forward against
the sleet to get to the warmth of the office; he had worked
out complex problems here that, even if he could remember them, were useless now in this era of total change. How
he had longed for retirement, for the freedom of Trelawney
that he had enjoyed during precisely four months! Everything seemed a taciturn gray as he hurried Lilian along. All
things were alike to him, the prospect of a new country with

its difficult period of readaptation, the "Sorry, there's no room for you" that he would probably hear at the airport, getting back to the country or even being arrested as he seemed to be one of the people the present leaders disliked. He had lost the things he valued most, independence of movement and judgment, so what did anything matter? It was as if he had swallowed an antidote for snake bite. The important thing was to get Lilian away and this stopped stray thoughts from entering his mind. The poison that was also in the antidote would begin to work on him presently.

"Is it very much further?" Lilian was finding the pace too fast for her.

"Down here, the first on the right, a wriggle that I can't describe and we're there."

The houses were shut and the blinds were drawn. He noticed too late a group of boys at the corner. "Say we are working here if they question us and are trying to get home." He was glad that he had put on his old mackintosh over his otherwise good clothes.

He thought they were going to pass. They were turning up the other road when one of the youths stepped forward and said suspiciously, "Where are you going? The Meeting's the other way."

"I work at the newsstand down there and I want to join my sister at the station," Lilian was truculent, "what's wrong with that?"

"Aren't you going to hear the speeches?"

"I'm coming back when I've met my sister."

The youth hesitated, he had the inevitable badge on his sweater. The couple was walking away but they both looked tired and ordinary and he had been warned not to antagonize the workers. "You'll be lucky if you find her in the crowds," he said, stepping aside so that they could pass. They hurried forward, Lilian managing now to keep up a steady pace, found the alley and came into the garage by the back entrance.

"Bit late, aren't you?" the owner said.

"We came directly we got our tickets. The sooner we're off the better."

"Money first," the man held out his hand. Robinson counted out the sum that had been agreed and thought as he did so that he would not have enough to return to Trelawney even if the trains were running.

"Bert!"

The driver who had met him so often when he had returned from business journeys came forward in a dirty overall. He was a middle-aged man with legs that seemed too short for him. "I told him to keep on his working clothes. You're more likely to get through that way."

"The bags are in the car, sir," Bert opened the door, "I'd like the lady to sit beside me in front. If you'll sit behind and keep your raincoat on, I think it will be better. And if we're stopped, let me do the talking."

"Good-by." The owner nodded, waved them on and went back inside the garage. Their former friendly relationship of exchanging a word about the weather if Robinson had happened to pass, was over. He suspected that the man had gone to put on one of the badges.

"Now," Bert leaned back as they drove slowly into the street, "you want to catch your plane and I think I can get you there, if you leave the route to me. We're in, well, say the middle of the map square here and the roads are blocked on either side. I'm going east because one of my mates told me there's a place where they're letting some cars through to the station. Once across, I know a byway that will take us back where we want to go."

"You know best."

"Don't be frightened, lady," but Lilian was looking defiant rather than alarmed, "I'll get you there somehow but it may take time. Let me do the talking," he repeated, "if we're stopped."

They raced down an empty road although Robinson felt that unseen faces were at every window. Places that had been as familiar to him as his own room were now more alien than the country where he hoped to settle. It added to their terrifying aspect that he could not remember how they had once looked. Sometimes a familiarity of line evoked a visual memory but it was faint; twenty years had vanished from his mind, twenty years of work and fog and struggle with only the promise of Trelawney in the summer. Could a lifetime disappear as utterly as this? It could, he supposed, even the moors where he had argued with Alex not ten days before had dissolved into mist. "You have got the tickets, sir?" He started at the sound of Bert's voice and took out his wallet.

"Oh, Mr. Robinson, did the consul give you a paper or something?"

"I have my ticket," he frowned at Lilian, "better get yours ready."

He had found a talisman in his note case. It was simply the cover from the last air ticket that he had used, a month or two before leaving for Trelawney. He usually discarded such scraps at once but it had stuck forgotten in a fold of the wallet until he had turned it out on the previous evening. If they opened the tickets, they would see that it had no value but if it were a casual inspection, he might get away with it.

"What these fools think they are up to is beyond me," Bert gave a hurried glance behind him. "These weeks are the best in the year, I've taken foreign tourists for a two or three day trip and had lots of airport work. I need the money, I've got a wife and two kids. What do they think they are doing to us?"

"It's so sudden."

"No, I wouldn't say that, sir. It's been in the air for years. But who did anything about it? Shoved the blame around but wouldn't do nothing themselves. Shameful, it was, shameful. Friend of mine was hit on the head by a lout and what did he get but sympathy? Sympathy is a hell of a lot of use if a man's out for a fortnight on half wages."

"People are apathetic."

"Plain lazy, I call it, sir." The car swerved suddenly to avoid a barrow that had been upset in the street. Two cabbages and a trail of apples, they looked just like a green plastic hose, had rolled into the gutter. "Wonder what happened there," Bert looked round again uneasily, "somebody they didn't like or who wouldn't go along with them."

It was really a nightmare, this race round empty squares with a dense, low murmur of voices coming towards them from the main street. Was it a symbol of the last decade, of a decay that could no more be stopped than a plague, was the Movement a throwback to some prehistoric beast whose huge limbs did not always receive messages from the tiny brain inside its head? "Now, sir, have the papers ready. If we can cross as if we were going to the station, I'll get you back all right for your plane."

There seemed little chance of any vehicle entering the static mass but there were no pedestrians and Bert swung the car round the corner onto the pavement. "Give us a chance, mate," he bellowed, "I want to get 'ome." A man grinned from the top of a truck and paused just long enough to let him jerk them into the line. "This is going to take us all afternoon," he grumbled, his eyes on a pram and two suitcases strapped to the roof of a taxi in front of them, "why do they bother to try to get away? It will be just the same in the country."

"That horrid little man," Lilian grumbled, speaking for the first time since they had left the garage.

"Oh, don't start that argument again," she must not let Bert know, honest though he appeared to be, that she was leaving because she had a cottage, or had had would be the better word, and was being dispossessed. "Let's wait till we are out of this tangle."

They sat. It was like being caught in traffic on the first morning of a holiday when a missed train would mean a whole wasted day. Only this was worse although he must not exaggerate, it was almost a game of life and death. They were literally playthings, Lilian had the visa, he had the chance of one, and here they were, stuck between trucks, cars, cycles and a stream of people who had just left a factory and were coming up a side street, some struggling towards the demon-strations and others equally anxious to get home.

He tried to split the crowd up into segments, the girl with cherries printed on a pale gray dress and the one in plain yellow, who were clinging together as if for protection, three youths totally uninterested in them, a man in a dirty overall with a paper under his arm, another carrying some heavy, football-shaped object against his chest, a fellow with a crippled arm. He had to look carefully from one person to the other as if he were following the pattern of a carpet, otherwise they flowed into a nub of heads. The minutes ticked away, sometimes they were able to move forward for a yard or two, then they slowed down into a dense, heaving mass.

They sat. There was no other word for it. It would have been impossible, had they wished, to open the door of the car. Robinson went through his pockets for something to do. They were surprisingly empty apart from his wallet, a pen, a handkerchief and his knife. His fingers touched something hard at the bottom of the one in his raincoat and he pulled out, not the coin he had imagined, but so ordinary a shell that he could not have picked it up out of curiosity, it must have stuck to the lining on some beach. He felt its ridges with his hand, he tried to imagine the day with the sun setting on blue, tossing waves, but it seemed forlorn and out of place in the middle of these people, trying either as they were themselves to escape or merely to get home to their tea. Every five minutes they gained perhaps a yard.

"They're turning the cars down a side street but back in the direction from which we've come." Bert stuck his head outside the window, he was visibly worried. A group of men with armlets round their sleeves were standing in the middle of the road.

The cars in front of them stopped. Somebody hooted behind them but nobody could move. It was an impasse such as he had known to happen in life when the hours passed into days and movement was blocked by extraneous things. Robin-

son looked at his watch, it was ten minutes to six. His nerves
prickled under his sleeves, death would be preferable to the
torture of sitting here. He pulled back his cuff and glanced
down, was it possible that only a minute had passed? A clock
in a post office window gave precisely the same time. Bert's
lips moved and he knew that he was swearing. The only
sign of nervousness that Lilian showed was that her hands,
they were usually open on her lap, were tightly clenched.

A taxi in front of them halted; after a moment or two, the
driver turned back down the adjacent road. Then it was their
turn. "What are you doing here?" the guard said insolently,
"Can't you read? Don't you know that all traffic has been
stopped?"

"Except for the station, sir."

"Who said you could go to the station?"

"Your Control at Winchester Road. They don't live here,"
Bert jerked his head towards his passengers.

"Who are they? Foreigners?"

"No, Colonials."

"Doing a bunk for the bush," the man smiled at his own
joke, "but there are no trains running."

"Oh, yes, there are," Lilian, to everyone's surprise, held
out her ticket. "There's one for the airport."

"Diplomatic, I suppose. Well, if Control let you through,
I suppose you can cross but you know, driver, you won't get
back tonight."

"I can park the bus at the station and walk," Bert leaned forward so that the man could see the badge on his coat, "I don't want to miss the speeches."

"All right then," he waved them forward and they edged their way slowly across the by now thinning stream of people going down the main road. "Don't look back," Bert grunted as soon as they were out of earshot. "He's still suspicious of us."

"Lilian, you were magnificent!"

"If I make up my mind to move, I do not intend to be thwarted."

"We were lucky. I know the traffic was getting snarled up but suppose he had asked to see our passports?"

"That's why I said you were Colonials. You couldn't have passed as foreigners."

"I wonder if there are blocks on the by-pass as well?"

"We shall soon find out." After the waiting of the past two hours, the car seemed to shoot forward almost at racing speed through the bare, empty streets. The houses were closed but occasionally a face, always that of a woman or a child, looked down from a top window. The cats and dogs had disappeared but there was a distant, continuous whine from loudspeakers and whistles. Bert avoided the straight roads, he went down one route, almost circled a forgotten square with three plane trees and a lilac bush standing in the middle of an untidy garden, turned up a terrace and passed by a yard full of parked trucks. The district seemed to have survived from an earlier age, the bricks were no longer red but the dingy color of a piece of cake that even the sparrows disdained and as one crumbling dwelling succeeded the other, Robinson could not help wondering if the badges the men were wearing, as the demonstrators stamped down the roads not a quarter of a mile beyond them, had not been born from the frustrations of those attics and basements? "There's going to be another tricky bit," Bert grunted, "we've got to cross the Westerham road."

It was more open, a few people were walking briskly along the pavements and they were now too far away to hear the marchers. "Are they stopping cars ahead?" Bert slowed down as a man on a cycle came towards them.

"Saw nobody."

"There's a road block in front of the bridge." An errand boy strolled over from the pavement and stared at the car.

"I've got to get these people to the airport but I don't actually need to cross the river."

"I can take you round a back way," the boy volunteered.

"Hop in then," Bert nodded and Robinson opened the door. The boy, delighted at the adventure, leaned forward to give directions as they moved off. "Turn here, take the first on the right and then we go straight for a bit."

"Why, that's where May lived!" Lilian pointed to a narrow house, identical with the twenty others in the row, as they shot down the street. She turned back to look at it but they were going fast and Robinson was not sure if he had noticed the particular building that she had meant.

"I came up on a three day excursion with my aunt, why, I couldn't have been more than eighteen, and I went to have tea with her there." The city had been dirty and terrifying on that first visit and neither the crowded shops full of clothes that she had had no money to buy nor the theater to which her aunt had taken her had given her as much pleasure as May running down those steps and welcoming her in the familiar, Trelawney accent. "May went through school with me but her mother was a City woman and once she was a widow, she came back to her own people." It had been a November day and they had drunk tea, eaten crumpets and gossiped about the village in a room on the second floor. "It was the white curtains against those grimy windows that struck me," Lilian added, "May was so particular but she couldn't keep the front clean with the fogs." What had happened in that room during the intervening years? Birth, perhaps, and death? "She died ten years later," the moment of memory was strong although she knew that nobody was interested and she had neither thought about May nor the school secrets that they had shared together and that had once seemed so important, for a very long time. "She was doing splendidly at the post office and then she got pneumonia. She had grown up at Trelawney, you see, and she missed our air."

And that's her epitaph, Robinson thought, but he merely nodded. It was Lilian's story and he had no image to make it real.

The house where May had lived was now far behind them. They were driving a zigzag course again while the boy kept shouting, he was enjoying himself immensely, "Left," "Straight on," "Right at the fish shop," till they came to a wide road with a playing field at one side. "This is where I get off, mate," he tried to speak with the tone and authority of a truck driver, "unless there's a block when you come to Berrington's factory, you'll make it."

Bert drew up in front of a newspaper stall that, surprisingly, was still open, got out himself and gave the boy a coin. "I'll make some inquiries here," he explained, "we don't want to be turned back in sight of the hangars."

Sitting still, the old irritations returned; for an irrational moment Robinson wondered if Bert and the boy were conspiring to betray them? No, the driver was talking to an elderly man in shirt sleeves and the boy was walking briskly up the road. Bert came back a moment later with a newspaper under his arm. "It's just the local sheet," he explained, "but it gives some directions. It should be clear for another two miles but they've posted guards in front of the airport and nobody can get in without a permit. But the man in there says there's a footpath that the workmen use about half a mile from the buildings and he doesn't think it is watched.

You come out next the freight shed but I'm afraid you'll have to walk."

"Suits me, my legs are getting cramped," Lilian wriggled round in her seat, "but I could do with a cup of tea."

"Make mine beer." Bert was obviously tired.

The sun was about to set and the lack of visibility was comforting although it was not quite dark. Had the road always seemed as long? To calm himself, Robinson pretended that this was a last trip for his firm and that he would be back in a few weeks with retirement still in front of him. He read such names as he could make out in the dusk, Burnham, Fowler, the Ping Pong Café, oh, there was the little post office and general store where he had once stopped to buy a stamp after returning from a journey. Yet he could not keep his mind from racing ahead nor stop the unreasoning terror that came in jerks and ebbed away again. What would he do if the others caught the aircraft and he was left at the gate without a visa?

The posters on the billboards between the low buildings seemed more honest than the pretense of gardens. A round figure in an apple-green mackintosh waited hopefully at a corner for a bus that would never arrive. Tall weeds were beginning to hide a rusty oil drum, a splintered piece of timber and a cable wheel on the edge of what had been a field. "Here we are," Bert pulled up abruptly beside a footpath that Robinson had not noticed. "I'm sorry, madam," he looked apologetically at Lilian, "do you think you can manage the bags? It's the only chance you have of getting through."

"What are you going to do, yourself, Bert?"

"Make for the Red Lion. The paper man says it's still open. I shall stop the night there and if things are bad tomorrow, I live only ten miles away so I shall go home and stay there till this storm blows over. Thanks very much, sir," he put the notes that Robinson handed to him safely away inside his coat, "are you sure you have left yourself enough?"

Robinson nodded, actually all he had now was some loose change in his pockets but without Bert they would not have had even this chance. They waited to wave till he had turned the car and driven back towards the roundabout, then they stared at the baggage at their feet. Lilian insisted upon slinging a bag over each shoulder and grasping her plastic case, Robinson picked up the rest. "We still have forty minutes and it can't be more than half a mile away," he managed to glance at his wristwatch under a lamp, "I wonder if Alex is waiting for us?"

SIX

"WOULD YOU LIKE me to help you pack?" Sheila inquired as they drew up in front of Mr. Lawson's block. The words slipped out before she remembered that she had never folded a man's suit and she was relieved when he shook his head. "No, thanks, somebody must mind the car."

The street was empty and, unlike an ordinary day, nothing was parked along the pavement. Sheila sat there proudly, clasping a wastepaper basket. At the last moment, her handbag being too small, she had slipped the bills, a ledger, the cups, saucers and tins of sugar and tea inside it. She had had to leave the kettle, it was too big and besides, there would probably be a different voltage on Avalon. It was not her first trip in the car. Mr. Lawson was awfully kind and often dropped her near her bus stop on a wet day but it would have been nice to see his sitting room. She wondered if he had flowers in it? He never seemed to notice those she brought to the office.

Lots of girls couldn't have made a decision in a moment to leave their familiar surroundings and emigrate to a country as far away as Avalon. In spite of having worked for three years at the consulate, she knew very little about it. It helped of course having so few relatives. She had been brought up by her aunt, "My, but she was strict," she had said over and over again to Betty, her one great friend. It still surprised her that she had dared to leave the firm where her aunt had placed her, to come and work in the City. "I was afraid of Auntie but I knew I should go crackers in that typists' pool where you couldn't hear your own machine for the noise so I answered the advertisement and Mr. Lawson took me."

She could truthfully call herself a traveler. She asked to take her holiday out of season so as to get reduced prices and they seemed glad that she was willing to stay alone at the office through August. "I go with a group, you know," she had explained to Betty, "it's nicer than being alone." So once she had gone out to the Alps with some botanists and the next year she had ended up on an undiscovered beach at a new hotel that did not even have a coat hanger in the cupboard, but there were always the colors and little adventures to bring back for a foggy day or the tiring hours of the end of month accounts.

She must send Betty a postcard from the airport. "It was the last thing you would think," she had said to Mr. Lawson, who had picked up a snapshot of her friend that accentuated her glasses, her thin, straight hair and angular face, "the girl who sat next to me in the pool and who bought a new blouse every month, is still working at Fordham's, and Betty, my friend, went to the seaside with her parents and came back engaged."

"She has sterling qualities, I expect," he had replied and she had never been sure if he were serious or not.

And now she was going to Avalon. She tried to imagine what it would be like. If only she had bought that brown suitcase that she had seen in Miller's window instead of waiting for the sales. All she had was a tartan affair made of green canvas with royal blue stripes. She had got it cheaply in a country town after the driver had dropped her former bag on the pavement and broken the lock, when he was unloading the coach. The colors had not looked so violent at dusk. Would they laugh at her for traveling with such an object? And what could she say to her aunt if there was time to telephone? "Oh, a temporary evacuation for a couple of weeks." She did not want to alarm the old lady.

Still it was asking a lot of a girl, she thought, resting her elbow on the wastepaper basket. She was going to have to give up her room, her weekend walks, the easy familiarity of a self-planned life, for something that she had never tried to imagine. It had always surprised her when people came in for visas. They must have something odd about them to make them want to leave home. "I wouldn't have said yes if Mr. Lawson hadn't asked me," she muttered aloud and a thought that she had always pressed to the back of her mind, something that she had not understood (though Betty and the girls in the pool could have told her all about it), it was terrifying and wonderful at the same moment, rose overwhelmingly to the surface.

She was in love with Mr. Lawson.

What would he think about the suitcase?

"MR. MAGNUS IS late, Miss Willis."

"The traffic is something awful along Winchester Road."

Her chief had come down the steps ten minutes previously with surprisingly little luggage for so long a trip, just an overnight bag and a not particularly large case that he had stowed, rather fussily, inside the car. Since then he had been walking up and down the street.

The fool! Lawson shifted the briefcase that he dared not put down because the Avalon seal was inside it and tucked it under his other arm. Alex was a Temporary and had been offered admittance (with his record too) as a favor. Let him make up his mind. Have the guts to say, "I'm not ready, I don't want to try a second time, I'll stay here and take my chance." He must know that nobody would blame him, least of all the officials. What was inexcusable was to delay their own departure simply because he was striding up and down his room, wondering if it were worse to go or to stay and face the Movement here.

He stopped to stare at the steps that had been washed that morning and the two window boxes on the ground-floor windows. They would be smashed, everything would decay, the chain between barbarism and civilization was moving and, from his point of view, the wrong way. It was a pity that some genius had not devised a means of uniting the good qualities of both (for each had its qualities) and discarding the remainder but there it was and words would not stop what was already in full motion. "It's late," Lawson looked at his watch, he could give Alex five minutes but not a second longer.

"Would you like me to telephone, sir?" Sheila was angry because Mr. Magnus was involving her chief in danger but she could not help wishing that he would not turn up because if he failed to join them, she would have the journey alone with Mr. Lawson.

"It's too late." He hoped Alex would make it because although their characters were so different, it was impossible to work with a man for seven years as intimately as he had worked with Magnus without a sort of easygoing friendship springing up between them. Besides, the fellow was too impulsive to bear the yoke of the new regime with patience. It was doubtful if they would continue to recognize his official immunity, they would lump him in with the rest of the foreigners and there was little that they could do from Avalon to help him. He glanced at his watch again, four minutes had gone.

"Hullo!" Alex stopped his car beside the pavement, coming from a totally different direction to the one that they expected, smiling, not sorry, and without a word of apology for being late.

"We have been waiting for a quarter of an hour." How beautiful her chief's voice was, even if he were angry, and knowing him to be occupied, Sheila ventured a swift glance at his face.

"And I've been working for you!" Alex held up two huge white cards. "Yes, working, though I know you think I never do a thing. But when I saw the crowds in Winchester Road I knew we were in for trouble. So I rang up my attaché friend and he told me where to go to get these."

"But is the diplomatic colony leaving?"

"Not yet, but they are sending out their families and rounding up tourists who are foreign nationals. Look at this!" He pointed to the consular C on the card with the oblong stamp of the Movement underneath it. "Assembly is at the Round Point in an hour and we are going to the airport with a special escort."

"I wonder if it is morally right to accept a favor from them?"

"Of course not, but it's the only way to get there."

"You have certainly been efficient." He had been wrong in his estimation, Alex had much of the good barbarian in him, a swift decisiveness and an ability to think along unusual lines. He wanted to make up for his lack of charity during the preceding quarter of an hour and added, "You must be very worried about your friends."

"They left at a quarter past three and Robinson had hired a car so I hope they got away before the demonstrations started."

"What do you suggest we do now? Miss Willis has still to get her things."

"Leave that wastepaper basket with Mr. Lawson, Sheila, and hop into my car. It's small and easier to move in traffic. If you will go and get us a place in the line, we'll join you there as soon as possible."

It was on the tip of Sheila's tongue to say that she would not bother about her bags but she had to have a nightdress and pay the rent that was due to Mrs. Bolton. All the same, she got out with extreme reluctance while Alex fixed the huge white card inside the windscreen right in front of her seat.

"Mrs. Bolton!" Sheila knocked a little louder than the first time but still timidly on the kitchen door. She knew how much the landlady hated her lodgers disturbing her in the afternoon. "If you've got anything to say, tell me on Saturday morning when I've got time to listen to you," she had heard her grumble to people over and over again.

"What is it?" It could not have been a worse moment because Mrs. Bolton was in the middle of the wash. There was a smell of soap and damp cotton everywhere in the scullery and the tap was running.

"My office is being evacuated to the country for a fort-night. I want to pay you for this week and the next."

"Evacuated?"

"It doesn't seem fair to spring it on us like this." If she placated Mrs. Bolton by grumbling first herself, she fancied that her landlady might be less angry.

"They oughtn't to move their employees at such short notice. It's treating them like cattle. Why don't you go down tomorrow?"

"Then I'd have to pay the transportation. And they gave me the money to settle next week in advance."

"It's these foreigners, they bolt at the slightest straw, why don't you look for a job with your own countrymen?"

"Perhaps I will. Is that right, please, Mrs. Bolton? And may I have a receipt. I shall have to show them that I paid you the money."

"And I've got my washing in the sink!" Mrs. Bolton dried her hands on her apron and looked round the kitchen. The receipt book was on the top shelf as always, under the dusty tureen that she used once a year. Otherwise the dresser was clean although with the money that Mrs. Bolton charged, Sheila felt she could have treated herself to a fresh piece of plastic on the table. "Here you are," she handed over a flimsy scrap of paper, "now you're sure it's only two weeks? A lot of people ask me for rooms, you know."

"Oh yes, we may even be back sooner. And I'd always send you the money if it was only a day longer."

"It had better not be. I don't like my rooms empty, it doesn't do a house any good if the blinds are down all the time. Come back as you say and I'll make an exception this once, but if your firm is not back by Sunday week, you'll have to look for somewhere else."

"Oh, but Mrs. Bolton, I wouldn't want to leave you."

Sheila raced upstairs, six minutes of the precious quarter of an hour had already gone. She hated her landlady but it was a sunny room and difficult to find a place reasonably close to the office. She was emigrating! She couldn't take it in. She hung out of the window and stared at the dark red dahlias that the man in the house opposite, he worked on the railways, had planted beside the path. It was not that she was in the habit of looking outside; a glance in the morning to see if she needed a mackintosh or if the weather forecast on Sundays was likely to be right was all that she did normally but trying to pack what she would need and scrap the rest in nine minutes was so overwhelming that for a moment she couldn't move.

"It's impossible." How could a person change a life on the spur of the moment? Then she remembered the roar of the demonstrations that they had heard in the distance and she pulled her suitcase from under the bed. Its colors looked more garish than she had remembered. She zipped open the plastic wardrobe with its hideously large roses (Mrs. Bolton must have got it at some sale), took out her winter coat, her new dress and the four-year-old costume that was so useful on wet days. The two faded summer dresses could be discarded but where were her walking shoes? She flung things in until she could not get the lid far enough down to lock it but could only fasten the strap. A horn sounded below in the street, the quarter of an hour was up.

Her washing things, the pullover she was knitting, her dictionary and a map went into the little haversack that she carried on walking trips. She looked round, everything was in confusion and without even knocking, Alex walked in. "Come along, we've got to go, it will be hard getting through even with the card. Is that your bag?"

"Yes," she snatched up her rug from the bed, she could carry it under the winter coat. "You ought to cut a stag from a poster and paste it on." He all but laughed.

"I couldn't get anything else…" she started to explain but Alex picked up the suitcase and the haversack. "You won't want all this stuff, you know, the climate in Avalon is different and you'll get compensation and an allowance to re-equip yourself there."

But they wouldn't be her things, bought with coins that she had saved week by week and that were soaked with holiday associations. She must go, she could hear Alex clattering down the stairs, but she turned for a final glance out of the window. The office! But once they landed in Avalon, there would be no consulate! Perhaps after going there, it was the first time that she had thought of it, she would not be able to work with Mr. Lawson. The three years of filing documents in a language that she did not understand, the dreadful day when she had upset the teapot on the carpet, the phone ringing and the pencil stubs, all that she had gaily boasted she was glad to leave behind when holidays had come, shone out suddenly as the crowning happiness of her life, and now, but what else was she to do, she was leaving it.

"Sheila!" Alex was yelling from the pavement below and sounding the horn.

She dashed out, remembered she had left her handbag on the bed, went back, picked it up, saw her nightdress peeping from under the pillow, added that to the stuff on her arm, and tore down the three flights of stairs as if the house were burning round her. Magnus was already at the wheel, "Dump that stuff in the back of the car but get in. Punctuality is not one of your virtues."

SEVEN

LAWSON WAS STANDING beside the official who was directing arrivals at the assembly point where to park their cars. His heavy official briefcase was under his arm. "Oh, here you are," he said sharply as Alex drew up beside him, "I've been anxious, you're five minutes late."

"Mitcham Terrace was quite a long way off," why must his chief rebuke him in public at such a moment for being a little overdue? "We should never have got here without the card. Directly they saw it at the check points, they let us pass."

Lawson glanced round while he waited for Alex to have his pass examined. What a lovely evening it was and of how little value to most of the city's inhabitants. Half of them were terrified and the others worn out with marching on a still sultry afternoon with the bars and taverns closed. He was sorry to depart; he had grown his roots in the country without knowing it, although after a leave in Avalon during the early part of his consulship, he had minded the return so much that he had never subsequently gone home but had taken the annual holiday in his immediate neighborhood. Yet now, he glanced at the ribbon of sunlight falling across a ribbon of grass, this place that he had accepted as purely a duty had become part of him. "There are three convoys," he said, trying to think of practical matters only, "the first one has just left."

"Here is your card and number," the official handed the documents to Alex, "you are due to leave with the second convoy in half an hour and I must warn you not to leave this area as I cannot readmit you."

"No, don't move." Lawson got into the back of the car, almost stumbling over Sheila's suitcase. "We shall be at our position in a moment but I suspected unless I came to the check point, you would never find me. I'm afraid they don't think Avalon very important."

Coaches and cars had been collected inside a park, with the larger vehicles standing bumper to bumper along an avenue of trees. Lawson directed them to a side road where there were only a dozen cars and where his own was stationed, the last in the line. He nodded to the man in charge who had been pressed into service from one of the other consulates and given an armband. "Here's my colleague, we are now complete."

A bed of scarlet dahlias that were just beginning to fade stood opposite them. A faint splash of almost identical color was spreading across the autumn sky. "I can't persuade myself that this is the last time I shall see these trees," Alex straightened himself after checking that the card was firmly fixed to the bottom of the windscreen. "I've walked this way to the office every morning for so many years." Images flashed across his mind, the cream buds in spring that looked as if their tips had been dipped into mulberry juice, the squirrel scampering so unexpectedly across the grass, even the spider's web of intricate ice on a foggy, winter morning; he had hardly been conscious of them at the time and now he would be homesick whenever he remembered them.

"Oh, Mr. Lawson, I forgot to ask. Do we never have holidays?"

"Of course, Miss Willis, but I am afraid we shall not be welcome here for a while, I doubt if my country will recognize the new government. But there will be plenty of other places you can visit."

"Mr. Lawson," the events of the day had broken through her shyness and she could not stand the suspense any longer, "I suppose there will be no consulate in Avalon but shall I be able to go on working for you?"

"I expect so, Miss Willis, if you wish. It's flattering that you haven't found me too harsh a taskmaster. But we shall have to wait until we get there to make plans. I assure you there is no need to worry." He could not tell the girl, it would have embarrassed him to mention it, that he occupied a far higher position in his own country than as a simple consul here. They had been nervous of these movements and counter movements long before the actual citizens had realized their danger and he had been transferred to the post because he was a highly trained observer. His original appointment had been for three years but he had volunteered to stay on; the months had slipped by without his realizing the length of his service. It was natural for the girl to be nervous about her future and his administration would take care of her, "You really must not be anxious, I am sure you will be happy with us."

"I've had my bag packed since I got back from Trelawney, so all I did after I got the cards was to collect the drinks from my cupboard," Alex dragged out a canvas bag from the back of the car. "I'm sorry I had no time to get any food."

"And I stopped on the way here, I thought we might be hungry. It's ham for you, isn't it, Miss Willis, and I think these are the cakes you like, there's tongue for us and I hope you are grateful, Alex, I managed to get a quarter of a pound of your favorite cheese. We had better keep something for tonight. The buffet at the airport is sure to be closed."

A line of children played up and down the path, leaving was only an adventure to them, while their parents bewailed the baggage that they had had to abandon and wondered if it would really be forwarded. A man walked past with his two dogs on a lead, half a dozen languages were being spoken at once. The leaves were still green, there was a formal bed of violas along the path, the last probably ever to be planted there, the grass was neatly cut. Why was there so deep an urge for destruction in people, Lawson wondered. They used so much research to introduce automation into everyday life and so little to find out what really went on in a nation's mind.

A whistle sounded. "Off in five minutes, sir," the man said who had been directing the cars. Sheila gathered up the papers from their sandwiches and ran over to throw them into an otherwise empty litter basket. "Faithful to the last," Alex joked as she came back to them. "I'll take you in my car," Lawson said, "get in, it's the bigger one."

A second whistle. The convoy began to move and they were at the tail of it. "Still anxious?" Lawson asked, and his secretary answered truthfully, "Oh, no, sir, it's an adventure."

Sheila wondered if she had ever been so happy in her life or ever would be again? The slow drive, sitting beside Mr. Lawson, she was too shy to call him Roger even to herself, seemed to sum up all that she was. It was her long, lonely walks across the cliffs, the forcing herself to go to classes on a wet, November evening, that had trained her to make an instant decision, as she had that afternoon, when she had immediately agreed to emigrate. He couldn't promise, she knew, but she felt that he would arrange for her to go on working for him. It was all the heaven she asked, to dust his desk, take him the letters for his signature, make him his cup of tea and once in a great while, because she could not bear the strain of its happening too often, to be given a lift in his car. They moved down the long road that had been kept clear from traffic so that the foreigners could be got away and no valley full of bluebells, no peak emerging from a silvery, autumn mist could ever be as beautiful to her as these rows of identical houses that needed a coat of paint nor the little shuttered shops with an occasional field beyond them. How wonderful that they could not hurry, that sometimes they had to wait minutes at the traffic lights, let the moments go slowly, slowly so that they would last. She did not even turn her head to look at Lawson's face, it was enough that he was beside her.

"TIRED, LILIAN?"

"No, I'm thankful to be out of that car. Oh, I know we couldn't have got as far as this without it, but remember, I'm a countrywoman and I've walked all my life."

"I felt trapped too. I was sure they were going to arrest us at that road block."

"Whatever for?"

"Does anybody know?"

"I suppose they are people like that dreadful man who came to Rose Cottage. But after the demonstrations tonight, perhaps they'll calm down."

Robinson shook his head. Change was on the way and although, throughout the ages, villagers like Lilian with their roots in the countryside had been able to absorb it gradually, would this be the case now that the globe itself, rather than a particular part of it, was moving in new ways? His case and Lilian's bucket bag that he had contrived to sling over his shoulder grew heavier and heavier. They were not on a picnic at Trelawney. The glitter there of the diamond pointed spray would have tired them sooner than carrying a fishing hamper. "Life is a journey," he remarked and immediately felt foolish.

"What do you mean, Mr. Robinson? I should have said after today that it was merely a waiting room."

"Why, there's the main road or a road." On an ordinary evening they could not have crossed it safely for the buses but now Robinson felt for the first time the full impact of the City's dislocation in its emptiness. The brilliant facades were dark although there was the occasional roar as a jet took off from a runway. They were trying to escape from what to where? He looked up and down and presently saw guards. He guessed that they wore badges although he could not see them in the darkness. Then he thought of being locked up in a dirty cell and shivered.

"Oh, there you are," a car drew up beside them, "now don't tell me you hiked here with all that luggage."

"Alex!"

"Get in. I've had my adventures too but I can tell you about them afterwards. I shall feel much happier when we're all three inside the airport. They've got a gang in front of the main door examining credentials. I shall say you are consular staff."

"Oh, Alex, it is good of you to look for us."

"I found you hadn't arrived and then slipped out again on the pretext of putting the car in the garage. Those idiots are taking the whole place over at midnight but our flight is scheduled for eleven. They want to get the tourists away first."

Alex glanced quickly round at the dark, empty landscape. There was nothing to be seen except pylons and a net of runway lights. How mixed man's motives were! He had contrived to be three cars behind Lawson at the check point and once he had ascertained from the officials that two of the "staff" were still missing, he had turned back to cruise slowly up and down in search of his friends. He had been determined to rescue them but he had also disobeyed with a great deal of satisfaction his chief's order to keep closely behind him and he was prepared to save even a complete stranger from the Movement if he had the opportunity.

A ring of men in green overalls was standing in front of the one, dimly lighted entrance where a queue of people were waiting with passports in their hands. "Now, Lilian, don't answer back whatever they may say to you. And here," he shoved a stiff piece of paper into his friend's hand, "show them this but don't let Lawson see it." It was an embossed card declaring Robinson to be of Avalon extraction and a clerk at the consulate, and it was stamped with the Great Seal. "It's good," Alex grinned as he turned away to park the car in the garage, "I forged it myself."

THE PASSAGE WITH a single, blue light glowing above every door in the long corridor reminded Robinson of a planetarium. It was the section reserved for the lesser companies and the only sounds were their own footsteps and the occasional roar of a plane. They stopped several times to search for Avalon Airlines and discovered it finally in the middle of the block. "I'm safe!" Robinson looked at his pass before putting it into his pocket, the guards, seeing the seal, had barely troubled to glance at it at the gate. He knocked and entered a small lounge with Lilian following closely behind him. The row of blue upholstered chairs were rather shabby and the small desk at the far end was covered with dust. "So Magnus found you?" Lawson seemed amused and even friendly, "They say sport is an ideal mixer and it seems to be true. I ordered him to stay with me and when he did not join us, I guessed he had gone to look for you. He told me you had taken him fishing in the holidays."

"Without him, we should have been stopped at the gate."

"Better settle down for a bit, there are plenty of chairs. They are getting the tourists and the Big Animals away first. Our turn is supposed to come at eleven but I suspect they will be late."

Safe! Lilian flopped onto a sofa. Robinson felt a slight ringing in his ears. It reminded him of the sea and for the first time for days he could think of Trelawney without pain. Not even the Movement and its badges could stop the blue tides racing past the headland nor catch the clouds in the sky.

"Mr. Robinson!"

The tone was so sharp that he jumped up in bewilderment as if he were a sailor and the consul his captain.

"In these grave times, I am sure you will agree it is essential to stick to regulations. We know that one of the two applicants is on his way and it is possible that the second may still reach us. All the same, I am prepared to grant you the visa if he has not arrived by nine o'clock. You can then arrange with Mr. Magnus about paying your fare."

"Thank you, sir." The tyrant! He could think of no other word. Robinson felt the card that Alex had given him and that was safely inside his pocket but although the Movement had treated it with respect, Lawson would recognize its falsity at once. It was true that there were only ten minutes to go but ashamed as he was because the brute was watching him, he could not keep his eyes from the clock. Why did people speak of time being swift? It had been so during certain moments at Trelawney but these last days had been a process of total frustration. What was going to happen to the people he knew? To Bill with his boat, Bert and his car, above all, to poor Miss Webb? Would they let her join her sister in America and would the hotel recede in her mind until it seemed merely a kind of school? He did not attempt to take off his mackintosh nor add his bags to the luggage in front of the desk. He heard a step, watched the door open, and jumped. "Take it easy, Mr. Robinson," the consul said with some amusement, "you're safe, it's a minute past nine."

"All secure!" It was Alex who came in boisterously, "Though I don't know why I bothered, I shall never see the car again. I've brought what was left of the sandwiches and you've got the drinks but I don't know what we are going to do about getting Lilian her tea."

"I've got our office canister," Sheila's head bobbed up from the opposite side of the sofa where she had been repacking her suitcase, "if only we could get some hot water." Once she had made sure that Mr. Lawson could not see her, she had piled her things on the seat and by folding them carefully and leaving out her walking shoes, she had got everything back including her rug, strapped the bag and had even been able to lock it. She would have to find a place for the shoes in her haversack.

"Suppose we search the building," Alex was restless, "there used to be another buffet on the main floor."

"First of all, we must get your friend's papers in order," Mr. Lawson opened his case and took out an ink pad and the smaller seal. He banged it down on the passport that Robinson had opened and put on the table as if it were an exercise in balance rather than the rescue of a life. "Give him his ticket before you go exploring again. Can't you ever be quiet?"

"I'm glad I brought the wastepaper basket," Sheila came forward with her tin of tea, "I know you thought it was silly."

"It's your triumph." Mr. Lawson smiled at her and she ventured to smile back. She did not want to leave this quiet haven to mingle with a crowd of angry and frightened passengers. "I'll stay here, if you don't mind, Mr. Magnus."

"But may I come? I've never been in a big airport before." It was a waste of time, Lilian felt, to spend the last two hours in her own country in this dimly lit and forlorn room.

"Of course, Mrs. Blunt. I'll check at the central office that everything is in order."

"I saw Augier when we arrived and he knows that we are here." Mr. Lawson settled himself into one of the big armchairs, "Go if you want but be back in half an hour, in case they slip us in between flights."

"WELL, IT MIGHT be a National Holiday." There could not have been a greater contrast between the silent, labyrinthine corridors and the brightly lit, main lounge. Bags were stacked on seats, children were rushing up and down, a few officials were trying to keep order and people were shouting in half a dozen languages at once.

"I think they ought to have warned us. I mean, it's an expensive tour and we're losing the last three days."

"But there'll be a refund."

"The guide says not. It's an act of God and therefore they're not responsible."

"Nobody can foresee a revolution."

"They can," Alex muttered so that only Lilian could hear him, "but not the day it breaks out."

"Flight one hundred and eight... flight one hundred and eight..." There was a hush as people paused to listen to the loudspeaker but even so, the destination was lost in the noise. Two different queues formed up in front of the one door and waited for it to open. Alex took advantage of the suddenly less crowded aisle to advance towards the buffet.

"Put that bag down, Tommy, or I'll slap you."

"He's tired, I expect."

Three girls shoved themselves in front of Lilian, momentarily cutting her off from Alex. To her amusement, one of them had put on two skirts, and a green hem hung below the checked costume that she was wearing on top of it. One of the others was carrying several sweaters under the coat on her arm; baggage was severely limited.

"It was the most beautiful color you ever saw and the assistant was putting it aside for me. If only I'd taken it then and not said I'd go back for it in the morning. I didn't really enjoy that palace, or whatever it was we saw, at all."

"Never put off to tomorrow the thing you want to do today," Alex interrupted in his most serious voice and the girls nodded.

"Flight one hundred and eight... flight one hundred and eight..." An official opened the door and one file hurried along the terrace while the second queue wandered back into the hall to find the places they had previously occupied were taken.

"Let me through, please, let me through," it was the girl with two skirts trying frantically to get to the door.

"Hurry, miss, the plane's leaving."

Lilian wandered over to the bookstall. It had been stripped of its magazines, people wanted something to read during the journey, but the newspapers lay there in great heaps. Their news was stale to passengers in flight. She picked up a book on the countryside and read a few lines before shutting it again. What was the use of buying it now? She was beginning to feel the separation from Trelawney more than she had expected. At first she had been too tired, or preoccupied with the formalities of the journey, but now the lighted signs, the announcements and the sound of the jets as they left were all warnings that in less than two hours she would be leaving her own country, perhaps permanently. It was that horrid little man. Suppose she had refused to let him in that morning, would she still be in her garden? No, they would have evicted her, she supposed, in due course. At least she was going into the future and as a result of her own independent decision, but she could not keep her anxieties from rising suddenly to the surface and making the scene in front of her bleak and terrifying that, because of its strangeness, she would have otherwise enjoyed. She understood now why Alex wanted to move; doing things, even if they were useless, helped one to forget about one's fears.

"Mrs. Blunt," Alex grabbed her by the arm and pushed her into a suddenly vacated seat, "sit there till I come for you. Don't move away or you may get lost."

"Are they really going to forward my trunk?" Rather than jettison her toilet creams the lady had spread their contents on her elaborately overpainted face.

"I'm sure they will make the necessary arrangements." Remembering the road block and their drive, Lilian longed to tell the woman that she was lucky to get away with whatever she happened to be wearing on her back.

"It was my daughter who wanted to make the trip. I knew we should have been safer at home."

If only the woman would shut up, if only Alex would come. There was a roar over the loudspeaker, Lilian could not catch the number, but the hall began to empty itself and a worried-looking girl rushed up to lead her mother away. "Here we are!" Alex came up from the buffet with a tray in his hand and two satchels hanging from his arm. "Guess what I found! Two Avalon overnight bags! They must have been there for years because they're faded and one's got a tear down the side but they gave them to me to get rid of them. You and Sheila can have one each and we can get rid of that awful basket."

There was only a single light above the staircase but an official was guarding the entrance to their corridor. He nodded when he saw the tray that Alex was carrying. The darkness made the passage seem a tunnel with no visible end and Lilian regretted the bustle of the upstairs lounge. "Do you suppose all those people will get away?"

"Too bad for them if they don't."

Their own waiting room was just as they had left it. Robinson was asleep, Lawson dozing, and Sheila trying for the fifth time to find a way to get her shoes, a brush and comb, a clothes brush, her sponge bag and a dictionary into a very small satchel.

"You are five minutes late, Alex," Lawson said, waking up, and looking at the clock.

Magnus did not answer. He took a small bottle out of one of the bags and put it into his chief's hand. "A last drink and a last celebration, there's tea for the ladies if they prefer it."

Somehow the atmosphere changed; it was less the drinks and the rather dry sandwiches but having something to do and being together in a group with ranks and differences forgotten. The clock struck ten and, as if waiting for that precise moment, there was a knock on the door. "Come in," Lawson expected to see Augier but a man entered, in an obviously old flying coat although it bore no badges. "Good evening, my name is Owen, and you sent for me. I am sorry to be late but I only got your message at three-thirty and I had to drive a hundred and sixty miles. All the same, I should have been here by nine but I was stopped at four road blocks. They told me in the hall the plane would not start until eleven."

"Sit down, join us, and we'll see what is left in the way of food." The applicant for the last visa available had managed to reach them in time.

EIGHT

AUGIER STARED OUT of the great, glass window that faced the runway. To an airman, the lights following each other into the distance, the almost empty space in front of the building, an official yellow car that looked like a toy and his own silvery gray plane waiting patiently for him at the extreme left of the final exit, were a satisfying and beautiful scene to watch. At the same time, he was uneasy. He had been assigned eleven o'clock for take-off but the passengers were hurrying across the tarmac towards the last big jet as if they expected it to leave without them. A child raced ahead, a group of men jostled each other rudely as they got to the steps, a canary-colored sweater stood out among the dark clothes, and a woman struggled along far behind the rest, one arm round her baby while a small, howling child dragged at her other hand. No hostess was there to help her. No other traveler looked round. A girl's bag burst open, she groped for the contents and bundled them into her coat. A ring formed round an official who was ticking off each name on a list before the passengers were allowed to scramble inside.

There was no other discord in the otherwise placid scene. Five minutes more, the runway would be empty and Avalon Airlines would have the sky to itself.

Augier turned and wandered into the waiting room. The space under the seats was littered with dirty paper cups and torn bags. A woman was sweeping what she could of the mess into a bin. Nobody was about except a couple of ground staff wearing the strange, green emblems that he had noticed everywhere that day. "I was wondering if there were many planes in front of me," he felt that the men were waiting for an explanation of his presence in the lounge, "my departure time was fixed for eleven o'clock but there seems nothing now on the apron."

"There's the old freighter."

"No, they got that away before the jet."

"Who are you?" The man looked him up and down as if he were an amateur, strayed from his private club by mistake.

"Avalon Airlines."

"Yes, you are on the list." He glanced at a paper on the desk beside him, "But except for yourself, it's finished."

Finished? Did they mean for the night or, Augier was immediately suspicious, was the normal functioning of this airport about to end? If so, it was a pity, the approach was easy and he had always liked the place. "Better get off now," the more friendly of the two men said, "they're taking over the place, you know, at midnight."

"I didn't know. I came in this morning to fetch our staff."

"You won't be coming this way for a time," the fellow glanced down at the badge that he was wearing, "it's unnatural, our leaders say, for the people to pop about the globe in a matter of hours. It unsettles them."

"I'm proud to say I've never been up myself though I do work at the airport," his companion pushed his cap back to scratch the back of his head. "Closing down will make it difficult for you, won't it?"

"A job is a job and there's always work for us somewhere," Augier shrugged his shoulders as if political changes were indifferent to him. "But I'd better go along and see Control. My passengers are here, the plane is fueled and I can take off immediately if they want."

The pilot walked into the corridor again and paused for a final glance before turning down the passage that led to the administrative building. Why had he eaten those sandwiches earlier at the buffet? They had warned him in Avalon never to eat the food at the airport; it always disagreed with him. He had brought a lunch packet with him but the wait had been so dreary that he had sat down at one of the little tables with another pilot and said, almost without thinking, "Same for me," when the fellow had ordered, "one ham, one cheese." The taste had been indistinguishable when the stuff had been brought and it had made him feel as if he had swallowed one of those old-fashioned white cannon balls they piled up

outside museums. Yet he tried it again and again, out of reck-
lessness, he supposed. But then his duality always bothered
him. It had torn him between the sea and the sky as a boy;
now it was between the airports of the world and Avalon.
He must get his passengers away. It was well within the power
of the Movement to seize the plane and intern them all. He
suspected that they would merely laugh at international law.
This feeling of being trapped was unendurable when he
thought of his home. He could smell the wet soil of his garden after a hot, showery day through the disinfectant that
had been splashed along the corridor, he could feel the weight
of a spade as he lifted it out of the earth. "Strawberries!" Such
a shout would bring his wife scurrying down the path with
a basket to work beside him till the sun went down and none
of the myriad noises around him then disturbed the unity of
his mind. At such moments he hated even the shadow that
formed the pattern of a control board on the path. "I shall
resign," he would promise himself but then the wind would
wake him, banging against a shutter in the night, the cry of
the gulls would disturb his blood in some inexplicable way,
he would wander out to the rocks where there was nothing
but a scratch of seaweed already loosened by the waves and
sit there longing for the lights, the tarmac and the steady voice
from a tower, talking him down to a runway. "It is a process
of learning," was all the answer he could get if he talked the
matter over with his superiors. The next day they would give

him an assignment to fly the mail to one of a dozen consulates scattered across the globe and directly his plane was airborne, he would forget that mortality was division and uncompleted knowledge, and long to return to his home.

The lights were sweeping out in front of him in great arcs of gold. There was the sudden, unnatural quietness of just before a storm. He looked at his watch, he noticed another sweeper in a torn, dirty overall watching him as if on purpose, and he almost ran to the Control room with no other thought in his head except getting permission to leave.

WAITING IS A form of death, waiting is a form of death, Robinson repeated the sentence as if, like a child running downhill too fast, he could not stop himself. He tried to imagine that he was with Alex, fishing off the Ledges, but even memory seemed to have vanished into a dark, uncomfortable blankness. He sat paralyzed on his seat, knowing that it was beyond his power to ask Lilian how she was or even to turn his head towards the door.

Lilian herself was staring at the poster of a village. It might have been Trelawney. Two teenagers in blue trousers and checked shirts were pointing to a boat from the top of a harbor wall. It was unsupervised, tomorrow somebody from the Movement would tear it down, now at holiday time the people would march in droves across the sands without permission to look for shells or sit down beside a tuft of thrift.

It had not occurred to her that there was danger in delay. Mr. Lawson had said that they would leave at eleven o'clock and she waited patiently while one minute slid into the next on the face of the big, round clock above the door.

"It was late when I got your message, sir. I should have been here by nine o'clock, all the same, if it had not been for the road blocks."

"It was a fine job arriving at all." Lawson suspected that the man's suit had been turned and the once expensive coat was of a pattern that had not been worn for years. "I'm afraid your application papers are packed. May I ask you your reasons for wanting to join us?"

"I was leafing over a handbook when I came across Avalon Airlines and a man I knew said that you might be extending your operations." The truthful answer would have been to get a chance to fly again but adversity had taught Owen to be careful.

"It does not look like it now." Something about Owen's dedication and simplicity pleased the consul. The fellow was obviously poor but previously, and Lawson glanced at the coat again, he had been comfortably off. There was a simple explanation; once a pilot got too old to renew his license, there were few jobs on the ground for a middle-aged man.

"I've been a flier, sir, all my life," Owen said unexpectedly as if he had read Lawson's thoughts, "the clouds are my friends."

"I hope you won't regret joining us."

"Oh, no, sir," he was beginning to feel more at ease, "I don't like the ideas that are creeping across the country, I should never be happy if I stayed here." Looking back, life seemed a series of steps, like the bites he had just taken out of his sandwich. It had begun in a rough field on a summer day when the blades of grass, each the same green, each the same length, had stifled the enthusiasm he ought to have felt at the beginning of the holidays. He had heard a noise, a plane had passed over his head, not much higher than the hedges but really a discoverer, losing and finding itself among scraps of cloud that never kept the same shape for five minutes. It had not been long before he had earned his license flying a kite that might easily have dropped to pieces above the same meadow. Those were the good days when he had beaten the birds by getting into the air with the first light. There had been flying school (as if he needed it), the gradual descent from the big line to the small, from passenger to freight, until the moment when his own domain, the air, had been reft away from him. He, the pioneer, had been flung onto the scrap heap along with other old bits of metal. Whatever they asked him to do in Avalon, the loneliness of his last unsatisfying work was over and there would be no risk of meeting a smart young officer whom he might have taught to fly and seeing (he did not know which was worse) the indifference or pity in the man's face.

The minutes dragged on and on. Owen shut his eyes and, as had so often happened after a difficult flight, the journey repeated itself in his head. It had never occurred to him that the consulate might have forgotten him, such places took their time, but oddly enough that very morning the thought had flashed across his mind that they might be too late. He had answered the telephone himself because he had happened to be walking down the passage. He had leaned against the side door afterwards, checking the steps to be taken as if he had been warned to be ready for a flight. Then he had asked permission to leave at once on account of urgent family business, he had flung his few belongings into an old bag, settled a couple of bills and put his money carefully into his wallet. By four, he had heard the clock strike in the market place, he was on his way, the dank verges on either side of an almost empty road had brought back the suffocating feeling of a stretch of identical hours, and the miles as they slid behind him an unfamiliar anxiety that he might never reach his destination. All had gone smoothly until they had stopped him at a road block halfway. He was not clear what the Movement was, nor what it was professing to do, but the fellow who had yelled at him represented an arbitrary control whereas from the little that the handbook had told him about Avalon, it seemed that there was still work there for an ex-pilot. A man had only to be simple, do his job and not interfere with his neighbor and then the discontents and intrigues that had caused these disturbances would not have happened.

"I'm going up to the lounge again to see if I can find out what is happening." Alex was restless and had his hand on the doorknob.

"Oh, do stay where you are. This is no time for us to separate. And please sit still, all this walking up and down won't get us off any sooner."

"I am going to see if I can find Augier." This was not the office and he was a free man.

"Waste of time. He's over at Control, no doubt, trying to get us away."

Waste of what time? How could the consul imagine that anyone could think constructively in such a situation? Alex slammed the door and ran up the steps towards the main lounge. It was an odd sensation to be inside it. They had turned out the lights except for a dim, yellow bulb over the door. There was not a soul about, not even a watchman. Somebody had kicked over a bin and dust, fluff and the inevitable cardboard cups had sprawled across a corner.

Suppose it was too late after all? The foreigners from countries whose rulers might protest and cut off trade had left in the big jets. Why should the Movement bother about the international rights of Avalon? He wandered into the broad passage that ran along the building but faced the

road and not the runways, to stare at the fields and the out-
line of the tunnel that normally divided the cars into streams
before they joined the traffic on the way back to the City but
the whole place was empty and dark. It was the helplessness
of it all, the helplessness...

It was not imagination to say that the taste of failure was
in his mouth. He had no enthusiasm to sustain him, everything was different from his first, exuberant flight. He
knew, as the others did not, about the difficulties of readaptation and acceptance, the little details that were and were not
like their habitual life, the values that counted in Avalon and
that were different from the ones, say, in Trelawney. "You
were too impulsive," they had said, "you must think things
out." Oh well, he had made his mistakes but as he had often
grumbled to Lawson, "Nobody there understands how a man
feels." Suppose he slipped out to the garage, took his car and
drove to the country, couldn't he find a quiet place where he
could appear to swim along with the Movement without actually joining it and live out his life in peace? He had a bundle of notes in the pocket of his overcoat and they would be
of no use to him anywhere else. "Nobody understood..." and
the consul had not understood either, "it was all so dull."

The window was open, there was a strange, distant thump.
A green, slightly uneven mass, it really did move in segments
like a caterpillar, flowed down the airport road. It began to
spread over the fields, several parties were advancing from

different directions, they had sticks — or were they rifles? —
in their hands. Had Control forgotten them? Could he get
his car out in time? No, there was not a single hamlet now
that would shelter him, those hordes were like the protein
that might come from outer space and poison, so a friend had
told him, whole nations in a night. He raced back to his
friends, almost without knowing what he was doing. "They're
here!" Glass crashed somewhere as Alex burst into the room.
"I don't know where Augier is and they're marching on us."

There was another crash above them although it might
have been merely the banging of one of the big doors. Feet
thundered overhead and, beside herself with fear, Sheila
grasped Lawson's arm. If only he had a phial of something
to swallow, Robinson thought, to have been so near and still
not to escape! There was a sudden silence that was almost
more frightening than the noise and instinctively they drew
together and waited.

The calm voice of an announcer came through the loudspeaker as on any ordinary day. "Avalon Airlines announces
the departure of their Flight 117. Will passengers please follow the blue light and proceed towards the aircraft."

THE SPACE BEYOND the airport buildings was a flat, gray plain
with the darker runways stretching like canals in front of it.
It was curious as the party hurried out, impeded by their luggage, that the tiny incidents of the moment filled their minds

and none of them remembered that they were leaving their native country, perhaps for the last time. Lilian was wondering (of all things) if her china dog were cracked? She had wrapped it up in paper and her scarf. Owen had his eyes fixed on the sky and Sheila was ashamed of having clung to her chief in her fright.

A man in green overalls stood beside the steps. He looked at them sullenly and made no attempt to help lift up the suitcases. Owen sprang in and began to stow the bags away with the skillfulness of long experience while Augier glanced at his passengers to estimate their weight. "I'd like you and Mr. Magnus at the back, if you don't mind," he said respectfully to Lawson, "then I'll have the ladies in the middle and you others in the seats behind me." The man trundled away the steps and Robinson closed his eyes. "We are leaving," he thought, "but what are we going to find?" He resented that he could not have chosen a moment of time when he had been at his happiest, to immerse himself inside it, like moss inside agate, till he died.

"Please fasten your seat belts." The familiar command had a meaningless sound inside an airdrome that was as deserted as an abandoned playground.

The order to move came from the Control Tower through Augier's earphones although only Owen, who was listening for it, heard the confused sounds. The plane, a tiny bird after the immense jets, began to taxi along the runway. It seemed darker, perhaps because the lights were dimmed beside the passengers' seats.

Was it an illusion, Robinson wondered, was the terrible drive, was the waiting inside that subterranean room, simply reflections of some early fear? Would he wake up suddenly, as the winds died down, in his own little room at Trelawney? No, the metal was cold under his fingers on the arms of his seat, he could not have imagined those mysterious dials in front of Augier. "Oh, look!" Lilian pointed towards the buildings, the lights snapped on, racing along the corridors like a wave; faces, they were too far away to distinguish more than the outlines, clustered at the openings. "Gargoyles," Lawson pulled back the little curtain at his window to its fullest extent, "as harsh, as indifferent, as cruel."

"We're the last out," Augier said, glancing at his watch, "if we had had to stop till eleven we should never have got away." They waited. Owen understood but Robinson did not know enough about the mechanism of flying to comprehend the reason for the delay. He wondered for a horrible moment if somebody had tampered with the machine and they would sit there till a howling crowd surrounded the airplane? Then there was a crackle through the headphones again and like a boy preparing to jump over a brook the plane raced forward, gathering speed, till it sprang proudly into the air. Up and up, the noise of the powerful engines filled the cabin, and the hard, gold lights of the runway vanished.

The City stretched below them although it was not a capital with squares and avenues but a cosmic map in reverse. The primrose ovals, the circles of gold beads, floated on a dense, violet space that the morning might reveal as gardens. An apothecary's red bowl hung as warning at an intersection. Butterflies, but they were as big as eagles, clung to white towers. Yet underneath that impermanent beauty changing with the air, hatreds were stirring that were always nearer to the surface than reason, every house was a cell whose inmates did not know what was going to happen to them when day broke. Some would escape, others would welcome violence as a relief from their private fears, changes had to come as inexorably as dawn would rise but who could count the cost in suffering and terror?

"Oh!" Lilian gasped, "They've set it on fire." A flame shot up, redder and brighter than the lamps, somewhere in the center of the buildings.

"We must not exaggerate, Mrs. Blunt." Lawson, who was sitting on the opposite side, leaned across to look over her shoulder. "It's accidental, I think. Nothing appears to be burning near it."

Robinson did not know how the others were faring. His own head was a void. The flames, their present course through the dark, seemingly thick air, were as incomprehensible as if they had put a tablet written in some ancient language into his hand and told him to translate it. He tried to fix his eyes on Augier's coat, simply because the stuff was tangible and real. His attention had been stretched to the extreme limit of feeling and he was conscious only of emptiness that pricked like the pinheads of the lights, what had he ever done that had made him worthy of rescue?

"Better try to sleep," Augier said quietly, "we shall land in about four hours at Puffin Bay to refuel."

PUFFIN BAY WAS simply an airstrip, one low, red building in the middle of a collection of huts and two great sheds. It seemed a friendly place in spite of a sharp wind that made Sheila regret that she had left her coat in the plane, but the girl who led them towards the lounge smiled as if she were really glad to see them. "You have an hour," Augier said formally before disappearing into the pilots' quarters.

"Do you think we can wash?" Lilian was carrying one of her innumerable bags.

"Certainly but don't be too long," Lawson had taken over as guide, "they'll be serving breakfast in five minutes."

There was plenty of hot water and Sheila even managed to produce a pair of clean stockings from her handbag. "Do you know," Lilian combed her hair back vigorously from her ears, "this is the very first time I have ever been abroad."

"And I'm sure you never expected to come to Puffin Bay. Till this morning it was no more than a dot on the map to me."

"I am still not really certain where we are."

"Oh, you see it marked on timetables. It's a junction for a lot of airlines. The people seem pleasant."

People? The remark set Lilian thinking about Trelawney. "It's odd, you know," she was speaking to herself rather than Sheila, "things do come to an end." The road would be built, the village would alter, even Mabel would change. She looked round, the washbasin was familiar but there were notices up in several languages beside the door. "The neighbors used to say to me, be venturesome now you're alone, take a coach trip but it wouldn't have been restful, not with the money and the food being all different..." she put away her comb and added, as an afterthought, "I like my bit of bacon with breakfast."

"Ready?" Sheila tossed two used paper handkerchiefs into the bin. If Mrs. Blunt started on her reminiscences she would never get to the table in time to pour out Mr. Lawson's cup of tea and she knew exactly how he liked it. "I could do with a cup of something hot myself."

The table was set at the end of the gaily decorated lounge and whatever the travelers felt, the revolution had not upset their appetites. Alex had piled three eggs onto his plate. The waitress was kept busy bringing fresh pots of tea. Lilian wondered suddenly what the food in Avalon would be like and Lawson said, as if he had read her thoughts, "I think you will like our meals once you get used to them. We always need time, remember, to adjust."

Adjust! Alex swallowed a final piece of toast and pushed back his chair. The trouble with these small airports was that there was nowhere for a passenger to stretch his legs. He walked over to the window and drew the curtain impatiently aside but there was nothing but a wilderness in front of him, flat, tangled bushes and patches of marsh that would be buried in a few weeks under drifts of snow. What a monotonous life it must be for the staff! He was restless, he could not or would not think, his mind was a void that was swept occasionally by irrational impulses beyond his control. If only the mechanics would finish their work! The journey was irritating him beyond endurance; it was ridiculous to be tormented by these many hesitations, he wanted to land and face facts.

"There's still time, Magnus." Lawson had walked quietly up to his side.

"To be flung to the mob?"

"No. They would be glad of your help here. This airport is about to be enlarged and you would get your fishing, there's a lake a few miles away. Or there are other countries. I could get you a visa."

"I have made my choice."

"Have you, Magnus?" Lawson looked at him anxiously, "It's no disgrace to take more time to work through an experience and if it had not been for the Movement, I think you would have stayed quite happily for another couple of years at the office. Answer me honestly."

139

"It would be worse to start all over again in a new place."

"Yet you are still too restless to settle down."

"Oh, it's only that my legs are stiff and I should have been glad of a walk."

"Listen to me, Magnus, this is important. They will be calling us in a minute and then it will be too late."

"I'll take my chance." Alex walked rudely away and rejoined the rest of the party. They were sitting wearily in wicker chairs beside their overnight bags.

"I didn't have time to write Mabel what to do with my books." Robinson looked round the circle but nobody answered him.

"Is it a long way from here?" Sheila pushed her cap back nervously, wondered how she looked, took it off and put it on again. Lawson had passed her the marmalade but otherwise he had not spoken a word to her that morning.

"Only a few hours."

"Do we stop on the way?"

"No." Alex saw the amber warning flash on at the entrance and picked up his briefcase.

"You seem to know all about it," Robinson joked, more for the sake of contact than information because he felt suddenly lonely and surprisingly cold. "Have you been talking to our pilot?"

"I don't need to ask anyone," Alex turned on him violently, "this isn't my first flight to Avalon. You see, I lived there."

NINE

THIS WAS FAMILIAR, this was home. The clouds stretched beyond Owen's window in floe after floe of seeming ice until he remembered a picture of men urging dogs and sleds over little hummocks that he had seen as a boy. He wanted—for once his imagination overwhelmed his practical self—to slip outside the plane on some as yet uninvented machine and glide from ridge to ridge, perch on a pinnacle and explore the dissolving whiteness that here and there split lengthwise to show an edge of blue. It looked as solid as packed snow, there was a hummock rising on the left side in front of them and the sky at the horizon was a pure, pale green. This was space and he loved it, it was a scene that nobody would see again because the air was in continuous movement and none of these fantastic landscapes lived as long as an hour. The plane passed through a cloud with a bump and as they emerged from it a little later, his experienced eyes noted the ice that had formed on the tip of the wing. "How smooth!" he shouted at Augier above the noise of the engine and the pilot nodded, "She's easy to handle in anything except a cross wind."

Hard as she tried, Sheila could not keep herself awake. It was twenty-four hours since she had left Mitcham Terrace for the office on the previous morning without a suspicion that, apart from the quarter of an hour she had been given in order to pack, she would never return there. She wondered if there would be some arrangement so that she could let the landlady know. There was nothing of importance left in the room but there had been no time to tidy it, she hated to think of the counterpane flung on the floor and the drawers left open. Her head nodded, she opened her eyes but they closed again of themselves. Memories drifted through the subdued roar around her, the scratch on the desk where Magnus had dropped a hammer, that horrid metal tray for clips that she had always meant to replace, "Must find a nice box for them on my next holidays," the sound of Lawson's voice asking for the letters through the open door. Yet something was worrying her, in this state between dreaming and full sleep, had she interposed her walks across the heather that gathered the scent of the soil into its stems between Lawson and herself? Yet suppose she had been bolder, had suggested he come for a walk with her, would he not have sent her away? Why were choices so difficult in life? I did what I could... I did what I could... was that imagination or a whisper through the noises of the plane? "It's raining, Miss Willis, and I've got my car. Let me drop you at the bus stop."

"Comfortable?" Robinson turned round as much as he could to look at Lilian, "It's been a tiring day."

"Day! That is an understatement. I haven't had a minute's peace since that horrible man called over a week ago. One morning I was quietly picking my beans, then I had to pack and fight my way through a crowd of toughs, and now I'm flying, and I don't know how high up we are, to a country about which, as you admitted yourself, we know practically nothing."

"At least it should be quiet."

Actually, apart from the uncertainty of the future, Lilian was enjoying the flight. Why, Mabel, she wanted to say (it was a pity that she could not telephone), you don't know how easy it is, slipping along in the air. Her friend had always said that she would be afraid to trust herself to "one of them things." It was difficult to concentrate when all she knew about their destination was what the sailor had told her as a child, "A man can be what he likes in Avalon, he can breathe there." That phrase had fascinated her more than the rest of the story. Sometimes in the small, hot kitchen of Rose Cottage she had wanted to rush out to the headland, to the waves that sprang as from the back of a subterranean dragon to break in white cascades upon the Ledges. She began to feel that she was back in the village again, walking towards the honeysuckle that marked Mabel's wall, or stopping for a word with the grocer who was so afraid of the chain stores. "You won't get the service, Mrs. Blunt, even if the packet's a penny less." What was she going to do in a place where she did not know the language, the money or the markets? You should have made more of your capacities, somebody seemed to whisper in her ear, did you really need to imprison yourself inside four walls and a plot of land? There were times she could have gone to the beach when she had stopped to listen to a neighbor's worries (was it a sense of duty?) or baked some scones for the people next door. Suddenly, to her own amazement, tears began to roll down her cheeks. "Don't worry, Mrs. Blunt," Lawson leaned forward and patted her on the shoulder, "everything will be all right, you're just tired."

"I shall miss Trelawney till I die," she started to say and then, it was worse because the very memory of the place seemed to be fading in spite of Lawson's reassuring voice. By a terrific effort of will and with the physical force that she had needed to stand against the autumn gales, she stammered, but who heard her against the roar of the engines, "I wanted to be out on the Seven Seas, I never wanted to be in Rose Cottage at all."

The long white plains that might have been a new form of opaque ice ended in a bank of clouds. These dissolved into shapes that could have been a map of the globe except that the indentations were simply a darker gray, they were not like seas. Owen leaned forward in his seat. It was a formation that he distrusted. He had known thick clouds to form and make landing very difficult, particularly between one season and another. Yet it was such hazards, calling both for concentration and an instantaneous maneuverability, that had drawn him to the air. It was less the pioneer moments of his youth that he remembered than the long, lonely flights on slow cargo planes through many types of weather when arrival had depended upon his skill and he had not had to be responsible for any companion.

The drawback about flying in an eight-seater plane, Lawson leaned forward to touch Alex on the shoulder, was that conversation could be heard only if shouted. He wanted to say a word of reassurance, he did not think that his colleague was prepared for his second visit, Magnus was not to blame although he thought he was, it took some people longer than others to assimilate certain experiences. It had been different for him, he had been posted as consul knowing that it was only for a limited time and he had accepted the difficulties, such as they were, because at the proper moment he would be recalled and transferred to another assignment. "Are you all right, Magnus?" he yelled and Alex turned and shouted, he supposed, some conventional phrases, because he could see the lips forming them but could not hear them above the turmoil.

"The weather's changing," Owen noticed that the sky to his right had altered to a deep violet and they brushed through a small cloud that seemed to have strayed purposely towards them.

"Just a drift of fog, don't think it's anything much, we often meet it as we get near the coast."

Alex was anxious too, it was not like the smooth approach of his previous flight. He knew what his chief was thinking behind him. "You asked for too much, Magnus, before you were ready for it." Long ago, in the violent youth that he could hardly remember, he had dominated his companions. Now he wanted power again but for a different purpose. He needed to smash the ignorance around him, to make people understand what they were doing, whether they liked it or not. "I want truth," he muttered to himself, "and I will fight till I have it." Of course he would help those who needed it, Lilian and Robinson, even Sheila, although he longed to pick her up by the neck and shake her because she was wasting the years in a silly adoration of Lawson who measured her simply by the yardstick of her efficiency in the office. He wondered what they would say to him when he landed again on Avalon? Treat him like a leper perhaps, or send him on probation to one of their remoter headlands? Lawson seemed to have read his thoughts because the consul leaned forward and yelled, "You'll be all right, Magnus, it will go smoothly once we land."

They saw the ocean below them through a break in the clouds. It was slate colored and stormy, the whiteness of the first part of the journey, the vivid green sky, seemed to have changed to an overall gray. It was a familiar scene to Augier, he had been on the monthly run, with mail and occasional passengers, for over a year and the steady boredom of the approach was all that bothered him. "Could run in with my eyes shut," he grumbled to Owen. It split him in two, the lift into the air excited him when he left the island, he was glad and regretful when the first orders from the Control Tower came through the earphones on his return. It was like being a sea anemone, he thought, opening and shutting with the tides.

Lawson was becoming increasingly uneasy. He had not the knowledge that the pilots had of the weather but it was unlike either of his previous flights. He kept watching for the slight movement of Augier's helmet that would indicate that they were within radio distance of the land. Then, suddenly, they were in the midst of turmoil, the plane dived, Augier righted it just as Lawson was nerving himself for contact with the water, they rose but the clouds were tossing them about like a snowball from one side to the other. "The radio's gone," Augier muttered anxiously, "it was all right when we left Puffin Bay."

Robinson gripped the arms of his seat as another lurch started. The journey, waiting at the consulate, the uncertain drive and walk through the darkness, telescoped themselves into one abrupt flash, yet time seemed less a moment than a thing of infinite duration, as long as his life. They were turning over, fear actually was rising in his throat and choking him, "All of us have our fate," he stuttered although nobody heard him, "none of us can escape it." It was only the moment of impact that he dreaded.

There was a pounding as of surf in their ears, the plane began slowly to right itself, Sheila had closed her eyes, the fear that she would be airsick in front of the others was greater than her apprehension of danger. "I shall have to go down," Augier muttered because the petrol was running out, he would try to make a pancake landing but how long would they last in that sea, and without contact nobody would know where they were nor send a boat to their rescue. Why had he left his wife and snatched at the chance of making these dangerous journeys when he could have been working in tranquillity and peace?

The fog was black and impenetrable, the clouds swirled round them and beyond them, the wings of the plane shuddered as if they were unable to balance the weight of the engine against the density of the air.

"The runway!" Owen bent forward and pointed.

"Where?"

"Why, there in front of us, it's as clear as day."

"But there's nothing but fog…" he looked round at Owen curiously. There was an airman's fable that some pilots existed who could see through the sky.

"Let me talk you down... let me talk you down..."

What did it matter? The petrol gauge was almost empty, none of his instruments were registering anymore. "Suit yourself," Augier said, waiting for the sideway roll to begin again and bracing himself against the seat in an effort to keep his balance.

"Straight, as straight as you can go." Owen forgot the textbooks, forgot everything but the simplicity of his first hour in the air. They dived, the clouds parted for an instant and Robinson saw far below them, as they came in for a perfect landing, gorse bushes, the valley full of apple trees and a stretch of white sand.

ABOUT BRYHER

BRYHER WAS BORN Annie Winifred Ellerman in England in 1894. She was the daughter of Sir John Ellerman, a British shipping magnate, eminent industrialist, and financier.[1] The Ellerman family was based in London and Eastbourne; however, at the age of sixteen Bryher found her true sense of place while visiting the Scilly Isles with a school friend's family. There she discovered the Isle of Bryher, which she later described in her memoir *The Heart to Artemis*: "I have never felt a similar atmosphere anywhere else, it is drenched with age, yet of the moment young."[2] She thus renamed herself after the remotest of the Scilly Isles, establishing her identity as a free thinker and an adventurer.

During Bryher's childhood, she traveled with her parents extensively throughout Europe, North Africa, and the Middle East, which provided her with an unusual education, and instilled in her a lifelong passion and appreciation for the histories of other cultures. She was a voracious reader, and "devoured every scrap of print" from her "father's novels to the timetable."[3] As a child, she was especially intrigued with adventure stories, a genre that influenced the historical novels that she later wrote.[4] As a young girl, Bryher's most abiding fantasy was to run away to sea: "I was convinced that if I wanted to be happy when I grew up I had to become a cabin boy..."[5] When she attended Queenwood boarding school at the age of fifteen (her first exposure to formal education), she found it tremendously stifling and limited. In her coming-of-age novel, *Development* (1920), she wrote about the problems with current educational models that discouraged individuality. From an early age, she pitted her own ideas and actions against the stereotypes of late Victorian society, and it is safe to say that she spent her entire life challenging social norms as well as facilitating and producing cultural experimentation.

Bryher had no interest in becoming the "lady" her parents expected her to become. In fact, her life is a testament to her brilliant negotiation of the difficulties of erotic and social life experienced by women who cannot fit into ready-made gender standards. A pivotal moment in Bryher's life came in 1914, when she read *Des Imagistes*, a collection of Imagist poetry edited by Ezra Pound. She was deeply affected by this groundbreaking poetic movement, spearheaded by H.D. (Hilda Doolittle) and Pound. That year, she published her own collection of poetry, *The Region of Lutany*, with her father's financial help. Amy Lowell, whose work was included in *Des Imagistes*, became the subject of Bryher's first book of literary criticism, *Amy Lowell: A Critical Appreciation* (1918). It was Lowell who directed Bryher to H.D.'s first book of poems, *Sea Garden* (1916). Propelled by her deep admiration of H.D.'s poems (she had memorized the entire book), Bryher sought out the young American poet, who was living in Cornwall, England. Their meeting evolved into a lifelong relationship, and later became the climactic scene in Bryher's novel *Two Selves* (1923).

Bryher's relationship to H.D. prompted a break away from her family: she regarded the poet as the one who rescued her. Similarly, H.D. regarded Bryher as "saving" her. At the time of their meeting, H.D. was pregnant. Not only did Bryher care for H.D., who almost died of influenza in the last month of her pregnancy, but she also adopted her daughter, Perdita, who grew up in the unconventional family of two mothers. Though Bryher entered into two marriages of convenience, her most significant relationship was with H.D.

During the twenties, both Bryher and H.D. became immersed in the study of psychoanalysis. Bryher went into analysis with Hanns Sachs; she also encouraged and subsidized H.D.'s therapy with Sigmund Freud during 1933 and 1934 (the subject of H.D.'s acclaimed *Tribute to Freud*). Bryher felt that psychoanalysis, aside from its importance in exploring sexuality and the unconscious, could help warshocked veterans.

Bryher used Ellerman finances and later her inheritance to support many modernist writers of the period. Bryher's first marriage, to Robert McAlmon, led to the formation of the Contact Publishing Company (which existed in Paris through 1928), putting into print writers such as Gertrude Stein, James Joyce, Ernest Hemingway, Djuna Barnes, and Mina Loy. She helped Sylvia Beach to fund the Shakespeare and Company bookshop in Paris, and with H.D., she arranged to have Marianne Moore's first book of poems published. (Bryher had an intimate relationship with Moore for the rest of her life, frequently sending letters, gifts, and money to both Moore and her mother.) As such, Bryher became an important figure in the fostering of experimental work as well as of the female modernists and lesbians of the Left Bank. While Ezra Pound has been granted full credit for encouraging and sponsoring the work of other writers, Bryher's generosity and synergistic impact has yet to be fully acknowledged.

Bryher's own writing career included the publication of two romans à clef, three memoirs, the futuristic allegory *Visa for Avalon*, two volumes of poetry, and eight highly acclaimed historical novels, which include *The Fourteenth of October* (1952), *The Player's Boy* (1953), *Roman Wall* (1954), *Gate to the Sea* (1958), *Ruan* (1960), *Coin of Carthage* (1963), *This January Tale* (1966), and *The Colors of Vaud* (1969). However, only the coming-of-age novels, *Development* and

Two Selves, reissued in one volume by the University of Wisconsin, are now in print.

In 1927, Bryher and H.D. met Kenneth Macpherson. H.D. and Macpherson became lovers, and after Bryher divorced McAlmon, she married Macpherson. Until 1939, the trio lived in Territet, Switzerland, sharing Bryher's "Kenwin," a Bauhaus-style home, which was designed by Le Corbusier. From 1927 to 1933, they edited *Close Up,* the first film journal in English. During this period, Bryher crossed the border to Berlin and experienced the aesthetic diversity of Weimar culture as well as its lively subcultures. The "twin birth" of psychoanalysis and cinema provided Bryher and her set with the mechanisms to more astutely explore the visual expressions of sexual, gender, and race identifications. *Close Up* featured the first English translations of Sergei Eisenstein, published many modernist writers, and grappled with avant-garde film aesthetics, psychoanalysis, and racial politics in filmmaking. Bryher herself contributed articles on the politics of film—addressing censorship issues, ways to make film more available through the development of cinema "clubs," and film editing (which in part led to her book in 1929, *Film Problems in Soviet Russia*). At this time, she was also involved with the production of several films, among them *Borderline* (1930), in which she played a cigar-smoking manager of the "border" hotel, acting alongside H.D. and Eslanda and Paul Robeson. The film explored racial borders and psychic breakdown through a style which featured quick cutting and editing methods influenced by Soviet as well as German filmmakers.

Close Up shut down in 1933 with Hitler's rise to power. In 1935, Bryher took over *Life and Letters,* merging it with *London Mercury* to create *Life and Letters To-day,* which published many important writers ranging from Franz Kafka, André Gide, and Paul Valéry to Muriel Rukeyser, the young Elizabeth Bishop, and Edith Sitwell.

In the ensuing years before World War II, Bryher became more deeply engaged in politics, and in fact used her house in Switzerland as a "receiving station" for over 100 Jewish and German adults and children fleeing Nazi Germany and Austria, offering shelter and securing visas for emigration. In 1940, when all foreigners were expelled from Switzerland, Bryher herself was forced to move to London, where she lived with H.D. and Perdita through the blitz (the subject of her novel, *Beowulf*). Although H.D. and Bryher lived separately after the end of World War II, their relationship continued until H.D.'s death in 1961.

From 1946 until her death in 1983, Bryher resided at Kenwin and took multiple journeys to London and to the United States to visit Perdita and her family, along with other friends. It was during this period that Bryher truly matured as a novelist. Her numerous well-received historical novels, traversing many different periods, represent her main genre for making sense of the political and historical upheavals she witnessed, and they reflect her gifts for psychological depiction and for transforming the past into a vivid, visionary experience.

During World War II, Bryher renewed her friendship with Norman Holmes Pearson, whom she had met in the 1930s with H.D. The Yale professor, who eventually facilitated the housing of H.D.'s papers, as well as Bryher's, at the Beinecke Rare Book and Manuscript Library, corresponded with Bryher extensively through the 1960s. Significantly, she dedicated *Visa for Avalon* to him with the inscription, "For Norman who first led me into the paths of Science Fantasy." Bryher's ability to see into the historical past accompanied a deeply perceptive capacity to gauge the future. Her own immense creative scope—as novelist, editor, filmmaker, activist, and critic—as well as her cultivation of other writers and thinkers are welcome sources of inspiration at the start of this new century.

Susan McCabe
July 3, 2004

NOTES

[1] In composing this biography, I am indebted to several sources supplementary to Bryher's own autobiographical writings, especially Barbara Guest's *Herself Defined: The Poet H.D. and Her World* (New York: Collins, 1985); Rachel Blau DuPlessis's *H.D.: The Career of That Struggle* (Bloomington, IN: Indiana University Press, 1986); Joanne Winning's "Introduction" to *Bryher: Two Novels: Development and Two Selves* (Madison, WI: The University of Wisconsin Press, 2000); Susan Stanford Friedman, *Analyzing Freud: Letters of H.D., Bryher, and Their Circle* (New York: New Directions Publishing, 2002); as well as the Beinecke Rare Book and Manuscript Library at Yale University, where I conducted my research of Bryher's work.

[2] Bryher, *The Heart to Artemis: A Writer's Memoirs* (New York: Harcourt, Brace & World, Inc., 1962), p. 141.

[3] Ibid., p. 14.

[4] Ibid., p. 52; and Bryher's biographical information as listed with the Beinecke Rare Book and Manuscript Library.

[5] Bryher, *The Heart to Artemis: A Writer's Memoirs* (New York: Harcourt, Brace & World, Inc., 1962), p. 17.

ABOUT SUSAN McCABE

Susan McCabe (1960–) is the author of *Cinematic Modernism: Modern Film and Poetry* (Cambridge University Press, 2004). She is an Associate Professor of English at the University of Southern California in Los Angeles. Her other books include *Elizabeth Bishop: Her Poetics of Loss* (Penn State Press, 1994) and a book of poetry, *Swirl* (Red Hen Press, 2003). She is currently at work on a critical biography of Bryher.

The text of this book is composed in Stempel Garamond.
Text design by Potter Publishing Studio.
Cover design by Lisa Clark.
Photograph on cover by R. Allison Ryan.
Typesetting by Wolf Creek Press.
Printed by Quebecor World.

ABOUT PARIS PRESS

PARIS PRESS is a young not-for-profit press publishing the work of women writers who have been neglected or misrepresented by the literary world. The Press values literature that is daring in style and in its courage to speak truthfully about society, culture, history, and the human heart. Publishing one to two books a year, Paris Press relies on generous support from organizations and individuals. Please help keep the voices of essential women writers in print and known. All contributions are tax-deductible. To contact the Press, write to Paris Press, P.O. Box 487, Ashfield, MA 01330; e-mail info@parispress.org; or visit our web site, www.parispress.org.